NOT HEAVEN BUT PARADISE

PREVIOUS BOOKS BY MICHAEL MEWSHAW

FICTION

Man in Motion

Waking Slow

The Toll

Earthly Bread

Land Without Shadow

Year of the Gun

Blackballed

True Crime

Shelter from the Storm

Island Tempest

Lying with the Dead

NONFICTION

Life for Death

Short Circuit: Six Months on the Men's Professional Tennis Tour

Money to Burn

Playing Away

Ladies of the Court: Grace And Disgrace On The Women's Tennis Tour

Do I Owe You Something?: A Memoir of the Literary Life

If You Could See Me Now: A Chronicle of Identity and Adoption

Between Terror and Tourism: An Overland Trip Across North Africa

Sympathy for the Devil: Four Decades of Friendship with Gore Vidal

Ad In Ad Out: Collected Tennis Articles

The Lost Prince: A Search for Pat Conroy

My Man in Antibes: Getting to Know Graham Greene

NOT HEAVEN BUT PARADISE

A NOVEL

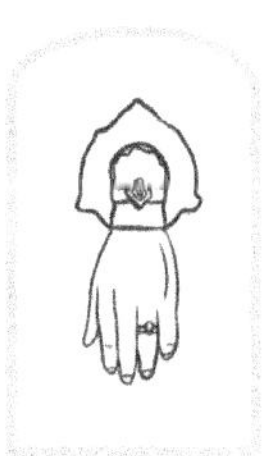

Michael Mewshaw

UNBRIDLED BOOKS

2025

This is a work of fiction. The names, characters, places and incidents are either the product of the author's imagination or are used fictitiously, and any resemblance to actual persons living or dead, business establishments, events, or locales is entirely coincidental.

Unbridled Books

First hardcover edition, 2025
ISBN: 978-1-60953-152-2

First paperback edition, 2025
ISBN: 978-1-60953-154-6

E-book ISBN: 978-1-60953-153-9

1 3 5 7 9 10 8 6 4 2

First Printing

For Desi Van Til and Katie Flynn, my daughters-in-law,
who made men of my boys and gave me beautiful grandchildren

CHAPTER I

The heat that had hammered Spain all summer didn't relent as the days dragged on into autumn. Paul Stewart raised the blinds in his room each morning, tense with anticipation, worrying when the arid season would exhaust itself and the weather break. The Sahara seemed about to invade Andalucia. Just east of Granada, an actual desert, the only one in Europe, was devouring acres of formerly arable land.

Finally, at the end of October, Paul woke one day to discover that snow had scrawled what appeared to be Arabic characters across the highest peaks of the Sierra Nevada. It wouldn't be long now before rain and cooler temperatures swept down from the mountains.

As the sun rose, turning the crenellated walls of the Alhambra from red to gold, Granada suggested shapes that neither man nor nature alone could contrive. Architectural precision collided with a chaos of hills and valleys that separated the oldest quarters of the city into neighborhoods distinct from the right-angled modern town. The scene was of such magnificence that Paul could forget that his bank account was at rock bottom and his life adrift.

To avoid shops where he had run up bills, Paul kept to the

Albaicín, the old Arab area of Granada. He lived in a vast, slightly shabby *carmen* that had belonged to his family for generations. There he slept and worked in a tower previously occupied by the family cook, Virtudes. She had always referred to it as her querencia—an almost mystical space where, she claimed, she was her strongest, truest self. The term came from bullfighting, Virtudes told him; it was the spot in the ring where the dying bull made its last stand, bowing its head as the matador bared his sword for the kill. Now the tower had become Paul's querencia.

Back when Virtudes had presided over it, the *carmen* had devolved from a richly furnished family mansion into a low-cost bed-and-breakfast that catered to students and rowdy tribes of hippie backpackers. Leaving most parental duties to Virtudes, his mother had had more than she could handle managing the B&B. Even as a child, Paul had sensed the fragility of the enterprise. Or perhaps that fragility had come from growing up among transient strangers with a mother whose mind was elsewhere after her husband, his father, upped stakes and returned to the States.

When his mother died, Paul inherited the *carmen* and attempted to attract a more prosperous clientele, not to mention a more interesting one, by transforming it into an arts residency. At first, paying guests streamed in steadily—retired academics persuaded that they possessed a creative side, weekend artists determined to discover what they could achieve if they painted full-time, bookish folks convinced they had a story to tell. To supplement its revenue, Paul registered the *carmen* in the United States as a not-for-profit 501c3—and with grants from private foundations and occasional awards from US arts agencies, the residency remained solvent.

But then the bottom fell out, not just for Paul but for any business that depended on international travelers. First, the COVID-19 pandemic kept people from coming. Even after the vaccine opened up Europe, a few grisly terrorist incidents made Americans wary of Spain, especially its southern provinces, which were roiled by migrants from Muslim countries.

By the time artists and writers began to trickle back, climate change had turned the *carmen*'s un-air-conditioned rooms into hotboxes. And the demands of guests had changed. There were new "woke" exigencies, vigilance about gender nonconformity and a heightened emphasis on diversity. Yet nothing Paul did to adapt brought the number of residents back to what it had been before the pandemic.

He started to stress the *carmen*'s deep and evolving history. He promised to lead trips to Lorca's house, a popular destination with the LBGTQ community. He pointed out Granada's multicultural, multiracial, multireligious population. He showed his guests the tiny arrow that had been etched into the kitchen's tile floor indicating the direction of Mecca. The house, he told them, had foundations that contained stones from the Roman era and others that dated from the Islamic occupation.

Although he didn't mention this, Paul wondered whether Virtudes had ever noticed the arrow and recognized its import. Someone just as pious as she, just as committed to prayer, penance and almsgiving, had preceded her here.

The *carmen* now had another faithful Muslim under its roof. The houseboy, a Black migrant who answered to the name of Blessed, had slyly insinuated himself into a storage closet off the kitchen. At this moment, Blessed was probably crouched on the floor muttering the Fajr, the morning prayer. When he finished, he and Paul would hike down to Plaza Nueva to collect an arriving resident who had texted from the airport that she was catching a taxi into town.

Paul could have dealt with the pickup alone, but Blessed had a keen sense of ceremony and regarded all travel, especially an overnight flight from the States, as worthy of respect. It did no harm to have him along, and Paul appreciated his company. He also believed that Blessed's presence reassured guests that the residency wasn't some rinky-dink operation. It had a staff.

At present, it had more staff than paying guests. A middle-aged American who described himself as an environmental musical composer spent his days lugging around video and audio equipment and what appeared to be a feather duster. He called this fuzzy device a "dead cat," and he waved it at arm's length, sweeping up ambient sound. When he found something he liked, he arranged a camera on a tripod and recorded himself recording street noise.

Twice he had been accosted by the Guardia Civil. Once a teenager, high on glue, had beaten him with a stick. Nothing, however, dissuaded the man from his project, which he vowed to exhibit publicly after he edited it. Paul encouraged him to take his time; there was no rush. Art needed to marinate, and the *carmen* needed the income.

"It's time to go," Paul called. Blessed was already outside, spindly and ill-clad as a scarecrow, idly stroking the wrought-iron bars on a ground-floor window, strumming them like harp strings. The carbon darkness of his skin was highlighted by a background of whitewashed walls.

From Huerta de Carlos, they headed steeply downhill. Judging by its name, the plaza had once been an orchard owned by a man called Carlos. During Paul's childhood, it had served as a soccer pitch of packed earth, studded with broken glass and bottle caps. Neighborhood kids, the sons and daughters of maids and day laborers, had treated Paul, a blond yanqui with no father, as an outsider until he proved he could take care of himself in games and in fistfights.

Paved with bricks, the soccer pitch was now an esplanade constructed atop an underground garage. On this mild morning, bums slept off last night's wine on the concrete benches. Later in the day, people would congregate to listen to guitarists and flamenco singers, girls with tambourines and boys beating percussive tunes on wooden boxes. A snarky poet at the residence had once accused Paul of choreographing this folkloric scene as a treat for guests at the *carmen*. But music, like the splash of fountains and the scent of jasmine, laced the air everywhere in the Albaicín.

Blessed and he advanced along crooked alleys, down staircases scalloped by centuries of passing feet. As a boy, Paul had owned an ant colony in a clear plastic container. In cross-section, insects had scuttled up and down winding tunnels, never losing their way. He pictured himself like this in the Albaicín, hardwired to track his location anywhere in the tight mesh of streets. Step by step, stone by stone, the neighborhood was mapped out on his nerve endings.

Blessed seemed to possess the same self-correcting instincts and seldom put a foot wrong. In fact, he was often a step ahead of Paul, anticipating the next move. Paul assumed the Albaicín resembled the place Blessed came from. Not that Blessed had ever named where that might be. When Paul asked, Blessed left it that he was from "far away."

"But which country?"

"One of sand and hot sun."

Blessed was similarly vague about his age and family. Even his name was a bit of a mystery. He paused before saying it, then paused again when others said it. Paul guessed it was a free translation of Barak.

Blessed spoke a smidgen of English and Spanish, but the sounds that poured out weren't always coherent. Patsy, the cook who had replaced Virtudes, believed he suffered a speech impediment or was soft in the head, maybe brain damaged after thudding across the Sahara in an open truck and surviving the Straits of Gibraltar in a rubber boat.

It struck Paul as logical for an illegal African refugee to prefer to remain incommunicado. How could authorities ship him home if they didn't have a clue where he came from? And how could they interrogate him if he barely spoke any language they understood?

Paul imagined—this was his habitual response, an overactive imagination—that Blessed was smarter than he let on. He imagined that Blessed was a Haratin, a member of a tribe of virtual slaves who scratched out a living in the Sahara. He didn't have enough fat on him to fry a hamburger, but he was strong and needed no instruction in tending the garden in the courtyard. He expertly pruned the fruit trees, espaliered roses, and tended to an irrigation system that prevented the soil from hardening into concrete.

Paul imagined that Blessed was illiterate, but he never put him in the humiliating position of having to admit this. What mattered to Paul was that he was easygoing and had a sense of humor—an unerring sign of intelligence, in Paul's opinion.

All of Europe teemed with migrants like Blessed. They spread blankets on the sidewalks of Granada and sold mass-produced trinkets and cheap knockoffs of designer goods. Keeping an eye open for cops as they haggled over prices, they were ready in an instant to roll up their goods and flee with them piled on their heads.

By contrast, Blessed seemed relaxed, standing outside an Italian *gelateria* shaking a paper cup, and singing, "Change, change." Rather than begging, he might have been cheerfully commenting on Granada. The city was changing. Everywhere you looked, Islam was invading.

Paul had fair hair and a slightly ginger-colored beard, and when Blessed first spotted him, he called out, "*Hola, rubio*," meaning "Hello, blond." He patted his own coarse hair, which was plaited in cornrows and tinted orange at the tips with lemon juice.

Paul smiled and dropped a euro into the paper cup. The next time they crossed paths, he gave Blessed two euros. The third time, they greeted one another as fellow *rubio*s and shook hands. Blessed's palm was pink and looked tender, but it had a work-hardened, sandpapery texture. They talked. Or tried to talk. Phrases in Spanish and English slithered between them, followed on Blessed's part by laughter and lapses into pantomime. The Black man's smile brightened everything except his eyes, which retained the wariness of a feral cat.

Paul gathered that Blessed had washed ashore at a Mediterranean beach resort and headed inland, where migrants weren't hounded as they were along the coast. Lacking money and papers, even a basic ID, he lived in a house with other refugees. A house or a church—it was hard for Paul to tell which. He assumed it might be a place run by Caritas. When he asked for the address, Blessed gestured in no particular direction. Maybe he didn't know the address. Maybe he actually slept rough in the street.

Rather than continue dropping coins into the paper cup, Paul invited him to the *carmen* and paid him out of petty cash to do odd jobs. Useful and unobtrusive, Blessed withdrew whenever he intuited that residents would rather not have him around. In the beginning, he departed at the end of the day, but eventually he lingered longer and longer, helping Patsy clear the dinner table and wash dishes. He ate leftovers from the communal meals, and after Patsy went home, he began bedding down in the kitchen supply closet.

Patsy, of course, was aware that Blessed had moved in, but she didn't mention this to Paul, who had already noticed and said nothing. He paid Blessed more than the going rate for off-the-books work. That eased his conscience a bit. By not declaring Blessed an official employee, he distanced himself in case of trouble and was consoled that the supply closet was safer and more comfortable than where Blessed had been sleeping.

Paul thought he knew how it felt to be a refugee. Despite his Spanish and American passports, he never felt altogether at home anyplace except the tower. As a child, on court-mandated visits to his father in Florida, everything had marked him as a foreigner. At his father's insistence—he refused to pay alimony and child support otherwise—Paul had attended a boarding school in New England and a college in the same state. There, he had learned to give a pitch-perfect imitation of an American. He excelled on the college soccer team, spent most winter weekends skiing, and was popular with the plump, giggling coeds who ruled campus social life. When he didn't pair off with one of them, rumors spread that he had a serious *novia* in Spain. The truth was that women in Granada held him at arm's length. In their eyes, he had become too Americanized.

In his college yearbook, beside his snapshot, was a class prophecy predicting that Paul would become a narc for the Drug Enforcement Agency. This had caused him to wonder whether anyone had heard about his father's alleged links to undercover intelligence. But it turned out to be a lame joke alluding to Paul's refusal to smuggle ziplock bags of Spanish hash back to his classmates.

• • •

As Blessed and he pressed downhill through the Albaicín, they encountered just one person climbing up—a stout old woman, burdened by string bags, breathing hoarsely through the stiff whiskers of her nose. Blessed offered her a hand at an especially steep staircase, but she brushed past him.

At intervals, the alley opened onto miniature plazas, more like private rooms than public squares. Families lounged under bowers of bougainvillea and potted geraniums. The smells of woodsmoke, toasted bread, and *café con leche* called to Paul's mind winter mornings when Virtudes had treated him to a *gota* of coffee in his glass of warm milk. Her skin, he remembered, had exuded the sweet vanilla scent of Maja soap.

What he remembered of his mother was always mixed with her anger and impatience as she interrogated him about his father. After each court-decreed visit, Paul was obliged to provide her with a report. Then, during his visits to Florida, his father cross-examined him about his former wife. Trapped in the role of double agent, Paul passed his childhood in fear that he could never satisfy either parent.

In a courtyard, a frantic canary screeched and flitted about its cage, while a wild green parrot gripped the wire with lethal talons. To Paul, it looked like the parrot was trying to attack the canary. Blessed clapped his hands, putting the parrot to flight.

Then they rounded a corner and Andalucia abruptly disappeared, replaced by North Africa. They might have been in Tunis or Marrakech. Saffron, cumin, coriander, and cardamom were heaped for sale in burlap sacks, the air redolent of exotic herbs and spices. Vendors hawked powders labeled as miraculous cures for stomach cancers, insomnia, and nocturnal terror. The soundtrack switched from flamenco to Koranic chanting. Instead of sombreros and castanets, souvenir shops sold tarbooshes and slave bracelets, harem pants and camel halters. US college girls lined up to have henna arabesques sketched on their hands. Boys rolled up their sleeves and had strands of barbed wire tattooed around their biceps.

Dubbed Little Morocco, the area was populated by stallkeepers from throughout the *ummah*, the entire Islamic world. Exiles from the war in Syria had recently opened restaurants called Damascus and Palmyra. And there was Samarkanda, which in spite of its name had a Lebanese, not an Uzbek menu. Given the enmity that existed among Islamic sects, violence seemed likely to explode between Sunnis and Shiites. But the terror when it erupted had struck elsewhere in Spain. A mixed cell of Moroccans, Tunisians, and Pakistanis had planted explosives at Madrid's Atocha train station, slaughtering 193 and wounding thousands. Al-Qaeda claimed responsibility.

Two jihadists died in Catalunya while building a bomb. The next day, a survivor from the same cell barreled in a van down Las Ramblas in Barcelona, killing 13 pedestrians and injuring 130. ISIS had taken credit for the atrocity.

Thus far Granada had been spared. For this Paul was grateful.

• • •

By the time they reached Plaza Nueva, Blessed's face was slick with sweat. Beneath a sky of acetylene brilliance, he gleamed like the mahogany African masks for sale around the square. At café tables, a few brave souls defied the heat. Others teetered on Segways behind a guide who performed figure eights in front of the Tribunal of Justice.

Paul expected to have no problem picking Simone Pierce out of the scrimmage at the taxi stand. He pictured her as a typical 212, not unlike most artists from her area code, dressed in black skinny jeans and a black T-shirt, her clothes packed in an army surplus duffel bag.

Instead, she traveled with a matched set of Louis Vuitton luggage and leaned against the front fender of a cab, her hip canted in a fashion model's slouch. She might have just stepped off a yacht, not an Iberia Skybus. She wore white slacks, miraculously unsmudged after a seven-hour flight, a striped pullover, and espadrilles.

Her light brown hair was streaked with blond highlights—*toques de luz* in local parlance—and swept back from her forehead, framing angular cheekbones. A faint spray of freckles across the bridge of her slightly crooked nose added character to a face that might otherwise have been merely pretty.

Paul introduced himself, shook her hand, and asked how she felt. "Splendid," Simone replied. "What did I do to deserve a reception committee? The cab could have delivered me to your doorstep."

"He'd never find the place. Anyway, it's just me and Blessed."

"How biblical."

"Koranic. We're very ecumenical in these parts."

She grinned, and wrinkles gathered at the edges of her eyes. Paul guessed she was more or less his age, in her late thirties or early forties.

"*Rubios*." Blessed patted the orange tips of his cornrows.

"He's saying the three of us are all blonds," Paul said.

"And why not? We've only got one life to live." She shook Blessed's hand, and he kissed his fingers and touched them to his heart. "What a sweetie," she exclaimed.

In the taxi, Blessed settled up front, his charity-shop T-shirt luffing in the warm breeze blowing through the open windows. Regardless of the weather, cabbies switched off the AC as soon as the calendar said summer was over, and they refused to switch it back on no matter how high the temperature soared. The driver shifted into low gear as if to build speed but continued to slowpoke along behind strolling pedestrians.

In back, Simone and Paul sat separated by her carry-on bag

and by awkward silence. Admission to the *carmen* wasn't competitive. No CV, no recommendations required. It was more like registering online at an Airbnb. To hide his ignorance of her biography, he fell into his least favorite role—a tour guide regurgitating facts about Saint Ana's church, a former mosque that retained Islamic motifs.

"I see I'll have to do my homework." Simone's voice was serrated with tiny teeth of irony sharp enough to stop him from saying more.

Along the Rio Darro, tourists flattened themselves against walls to let traffic pass. Arching over the river, trees shivered in gusts of wind that leaped from limb to limb. This route, Paseo de los Tristes, used to be the path mourners followed to the cemetery. Paul kept that nugget of info to himself.

"Hot," Simone said and plucked the front of her pullover away from her chest. "Is that a famous matador?" she asked about a bronze statue.

"No, a flamenco dancer. A Gypsy from Sacramonte."

"You mean a Roma."

"Excuse me."

"Nobody calls them Gypsies these days."

He couldn't tell whether she was joking. "Maybe not in New York. But here we have Elderhostels or hostile elders who flock to the Gypsy caves every night for a complimentary glass of sangria and all the cante hondo their hearing aids can abide."

Simone laughed. "You're so un-PC. Ageist on top of racist."

Where Calle San Juan de los Reyes tunneled through a wall, the driver braked to a halt. A sign in Spanish and English warned, "Physically Impossible to Enter."

"I'd like to steal that sign," Simone said.

"Fold your side mirrors," Paul told the cabbie. "We can squeeze through."

At a walking pace, they eased through the passageway. The driver muttered under his breath that just once in his life, he'd like to enjoy a woman this tight. Simone asked for a translation. Paul said it was a local joke too complicated to explain.

Whitewashed walls lined both sides of the alley. Cars had sideswiped the facades, streaking them with enamel patches and chrome flakes.

"It's like an urban art installation," Simone said.

"That's Granada for you. Always hard to distinguish creativity from reckless driving."

Cobblestones and potholes discouraged further conversation. To talk now risked biting your tongue or chipping your teeth. At intersections, narrow streets branched uphill or plunged down into cul-de-sacs. Between houses, postcard images of the Alhambra flickered past like a jump-cut film. At a hairpin turn, the road ran past a Moroccan restaurant, Chefchaouen, then rumbled around Huerta de Carlos on a corrugated dirt path that ended at the *carmen*. Simone reached across the carry-on bag and touched Paul's arm. "You're right. I'd be lost without you." Again, her tone was ironic.

While Blessed fetched her luggage from the trunk, Simone admired the immense front door, its brass Hand of Fatima knocker, its beautifully grained wood and iron rivets that bled rust like pitons that had been hammered into a cliff face. In the hallway, she exclaimed over the cedar-beamed ceiling and the ex-votos on display. They had been here so long, these tin replicas of body parts, that Paul seldom registered their presence. Virtudes, in her piety, had purchased them in gratitude to God for relief from various female afflictions. Breasts, lungs, legs with varicose veins—the maid had survived a Calvary of operations that she had recounted to Paul as vividly as she had described the outrages of the Franco regime.

During its incarnation as a bed-and-breakfast, the *carmen* had been furnished with distressed pieces of Spanish provincial. Heavy armchairs of machine-milled wood hunched on clawed feet in the library. Its shelves were stocked with novels and poetry chapbooks donated by past residents. Many books appeared never to have been opened—unlike dog-eared paperback bestsellers left behind by visitors anxious to avoid overweight charges at the airport. The fireplace, huge enough to roast an ox, was bricked up to guard against drafts, and the room remained bone-chillingly cold in winter.

There used to be a leather-bound ledger where people signed in when they arrived, then scribbled appreciative comments when they departed. Paul removed it when guests started complaining about the food, the isolation, and the expensive Internet service. But Simone professed to be charmed by everything, particularly the courtyard.

"I almost feel guilty for living here," Paul found himself confessing.

"Guilty?"

"I mean, when people are sleeping in the street."

"I'm used to it from New York."

They paused at a fountain where koi drifted like Kleenex in the clear water. "I read someplace," Simone said, "that 'paradise' is the Arab word for 'walled garden.'"

"Sorry to sound pedantic, but it's actually a Persian word."

"I guess I'm in for quite a learning experience."

"The water in the fountain is spring fed. It's almost too cold to touch."

She plunged in her hand, laughed, and snapped her fingers as if she'd been burned.

"A daredevil," he said.

"That's me."

They advanced under an arch of cypresses whose upper branches meshed. Pear and plum trees shaded a strawberry patch that sprouted a last bit of fruit. There was a sense, though never more than a fleeting glimpse, of lizards scuttling around their feet.

"Would you like breakfast?" he asked. "Patsy'll brew a pot of coffee and Blessed'll pick some strawberries."

"No, I just need a shower and sleep." She was tugging at her pullover, lifting it from her chest and letting it fall back.

"A glass of wine might help you doze off."

"No help needed." She shut her eyes and tilted her head, miming instant sleep. Paul seized the chance to study her face. She was a remarkably attractive woman, her skin so fine he wondered whether she had had work done on it.

"Once I have the password to get online," she said, "I'm set."

"There's a charge for Wi-Fi. It's not too steep unless you stay on for hours."

"That's exactly what I do. I visit chat rooms on Skype to find models. Just bill me for my time."

As they reentered the *carmen*, Paul pressed his hand to her lower back, to all appearances guiding her up over the doorstep, in reality yielding to a craving for physical contact. Instantly he pulled back, reminded of how often he had watched his father do this to a woman. In principle, he drew the line at sleeping with residents. In practice, it happened. And each time it did, Paul, like any man who hated his father, promised not to become him.

• • •

In the tower that evening, he lifted the lid on his computer, and while he waited for it to connect, he glanced out at the view, which would remain the same until the worst winter weather glazed the Alhambra like a sugar castle on a Christmas tree. That image reminded Paul of nights at prep school in New England when he had watched falling snow carpet the campus and worried himself half sick about the upcoming holidays. He longed to fly home to Granada, but his father demanded that he visit Florida. He could never guess who might pick him up at the airport. Often it was a new wife—his father had had five of them—or new mistress, always a coed from one of his father's comp lit seminars.

"Peter's off on assignment," the woman would excuse his absence.

"Off where?"

"He's sworn to secrecy."

"Sworn by who?"

"Langley."

Returning from these mystery trips, his father invariably brought cheap, kitschy souvenirs of the type peddled in every poverty-stricken nation in South America, Africa, or the Caribbean. He claimed that tourism was his undercover identity. He went so far as to churn out occasional travel articles. He once presented Paul with a snapshot of himself in camo pants with a holstered pistol strapped around his waist. The background of wickerwork jungle might have been in the wilds of the Congo—or just off Alligator Alley in the Everglades.

When Paul was older and rebellious enough to challenge why any US intelligence agency would employ a comp lit professor, his father barely suppressed his rage and marched his son up to his bedroom, as if to lay on discipline with a belt. Instead, he opened the bottom drawer of a bureau that contained a dozen or so handguns—Glocks, Lugers, .38 Specials—fitted neatly together like a jigsaw puzzle. For Peter Stewart, no further explanation was necessary; the weapons proved his bona fides.

One pistol was just large enough to fill his father's palm. It looked like something an escaped convict had carved out of soap. "It's plastic," Peter Stewart told his son. "Undetectable by airport metal scanners." He handed it to Paul. "Take it for protection on your next flight."

"Protection against what?"

"Hijackers."

Paul tested its weight. It wasn't much heavier than an airmail envelope. "You really believe I'll be in danger on the plane to Boston?"

"There's a lot of static about hijacking and terrorist attacks. This may look like a toy, but it has knockdown power."

As politely as possible, Paul declined the gift, but he kept the snapshot of his father clad in camo gear. It was somewhere in a desk drawer, lost amid the litter from his childhood. He had never known what to make of the man. The equally unanswerable question was what his father had made of him.

When he was still small enough to sit on Virtudes's lap, Paul had asked the maid about Peter Stewart. Her answer in Andalusian dialect conflated the past and the present, his family's life, and the city's history. She described his parents' divorce in terms similar to her account of the Reconquista and the end of the Islamic occupation. Blood had flowed through the streets of the Albaicín, she said, sealing the cobblestones as tight as the lid on a sarcophagus. The Christians had rooted out the Muslims like thistles. That was how hard it had been, Virtudes swore, for Paul's mother to rid herself of her husband. Afterward, she had retreated into the *carmen* and settled into a life of resistance.

"There was no surrender, Pablo," Virtudes said and leapt ahead to the Franco era, when Fascists set up artillery at the Alhambra and fired across the valley. The tower took a direct hit.

"The killing went on and on. Franco's men murdered my husband in 1947, years after the Civil War officially ended. Spain was full of orphans like you and suffering women like your mother."

Virtudes's comparison of his parents' broken marriage to the horror of the Civil War was more than Paul could accept. He knew he was no orphan. What did Franco have to do with his family? he wondered.

"I'm trying to educate you with parables, Pablo," Virtudes

said. "Your father was in fact a Fascist and a spy. That's why your mother kicked him out."

• • •

A chime signaled that he was online. Emails flooded the screen. Not one was personal; not one was easy to answer. The *carmen* was late in filing its annual 190EZ tax form. If it failed to do so soon, the IRS would cancel its nonprofit status. Putting Paul in a double bind, if he disclosed how little income the residency generated, the IRS might declare the operation a hobby, not a business.

At the end of each National Endowment of the Arts grant cycle, he had to report how money had been spent and how the expenditures matched the *carmen*'s mission. There was a growing emphasis on diversity, equity and inclusion—summed up under the acronym DEI. To obtain funding, Paul had to show how his arts establishment benefited "an unserved population." This demanded of him a depth of creativity that many of the *carmen*'s residents lacked.

After an hour of completing questionnaires, he typed in Simone Pierce's name and a lengthy Wikipedia entry popped up. It wasn't the sort of CV he was accustomed to reviewing. Her résumé glittered with awards and prizes, including a Guggenheim and a grant from the National Endowment for the Arts. Her paintings hung in major galleries and private collections and in museums in the States and Europe. She had had fellowships at the American Academy in Rome and the Rockefeller Foundation in Bellagio, Italy. With her credentials, she would have been welcome anywhere. How and why had she pitched up here as a paying guest?

He feared that when she realized the mistake she had made, she would demand a refund of the money she had paid in advance. Someone of Simone's reputation could kill him online. On the other hand, if he convinced her to stay, she might attract other artists—better ones.

He touched the Images tab, which brought up samples of Simone's painting, a career-long array of shock art. Every canvas was a transgressive, cutting-edge exploration of the human groin, clinically exact, skillfully blending intimacy and impersonality, eros and indifference. What rescued the work—just barely—from pornography was its absolute fearlessness, coupled with an uncanny subversive humor.

A passage from John Berger's *Ways of Seeing* prefaced a series of paintings: "Men dream of women. Women dream of themselves being dreamt of. Men look at women. Women watch themselves being looked at." To "deconstruct the male gaze" and "assert female agency"—these phrases coursed through critical assessments of Simone Pierce's art—she depicted enormously endowed men masturbating. The penises might have been helpless, hairless creatures being choked to death.

When she focused on female genitalia, Simone infused the labia with deep mystery and beauty. Gustave Courbet's *Origin of the World* came to mind, as did Georgia O'Keefe's flowers. The work wasn't without playfulness. Most of the vulvas were scrupulously depilated, but several featured sprigs of pubic hair, green and delicate as watercress.

Paul studied these pictures so long and so intently he ended up feeling that he himself was being stared at. Still, he didn't stop looking. He couldn't. Along with desire and confusion, he was certain of only one thing. He would do whatever it took to keep Simone Pierce at the *carmen*.

CHAPTER II

The night had gone quiet. Or as quiet as it ever got in Granada, where there was always the growling of guard dogs, percussive hand clapping in the plazas, the clatter of empty bottles hurled into trash barrels. Blessed had brushed his teeth with a *miswak*, a twig he had brought from his village, the one possession that had survived the crossing to Europe. Then he had washed himself as best he could in a pan of tap water. The Koran encouraged cleanliness, and it was crucial here. To be a dirty African in Spain increased the danger. In the heat, you stank, and when you stank, no one hired you and you lived on the street until the police slapped you into jail.

In the supply closet off the kitchen, Blessed stretched out on a pallet padded with the blanket that Patsy had given him. She had also provided a mosquito coil, which burned in a slow circle, its ember emitting pungent smoke, like incense beside a corpse waiting for the corpse washer.

Above him on the ceiling, a fluorescent light fizzed. Dead insects measled the long bright tube that he wouldn't switch off until he was sure he could sleep. To induce drowsiness, he had sneaked a glass of red wine from an open bottle in the pantry.

Neither Paul nor Patsy would miss it. But Allah missed nothing, and Blessed knew from the Koran, which had over the centuries been inscribed on palm leaves, on flat rocks, and in the hearts of men, that he was committing a sin. As a boy, in the madrassa plastered like a mud dauber's nest to the village mosque, he had studied the Book. He had never achieved the status of *hafiz*; he hadn't memorized the whole Koran. But certain suras hummed in his head like the bulb that fizzed on the ceiling. "Evil would be my drink, dismal my resting place, filth my food, the filth that sinners eat."

Among his iniquities, he regretted that he had never prayed at the mosque in Granada for fear of the plainclothes police who hounded men of his color. Jail held less terror for Blessed than deportation. The smartest, most resourceful boy in his village, he had learned how to read and to use a computer. Born with a caul on his head, he had been chosen and specially trained. Relatives had painstakingly put money away for him to travel to Europe, and he had pledged to pay them back. His plan had been to find work and eventually return home, if not a rich man, at least with enough wealth to build a house, marry, and have children. But here he lay in a tooth-yellow closet, crowded with buckets and mops, gobbling leftovers that would otherwise have gone into the garbage. Allah was hardening him, he hoped, for a purpose that hadn't yet become clear.

The curse of alcohol, Blessed had heard, was that as you drank, your thirst deepened, and you needed to drink more and more to reach that corner in your head where you could curl up and sleep. In the Book it was written, "Does there not pass over man a space of time when his life is blank?" Was this then that blankness? Or had he been lost before he set out on a trip that had lasted months and covered two thousand miles, a trip whose memory still terrified him?

The Sahara had swept through the streets of his village. Crops barely broke the crust of the earth before they withered and died. He obeyed his father and boarded a dump truck along with dozens of young men and a few women, all bound for Spain and fertile land.

The women clung together, anxious not to touch the men. But soon all the bodies, male and female, sank into a single undifferentiated mass. To anybody watching from the roadside, the truck appeared to be heaped with bundles of shabby clothes of the sort that relief agencies collected in rich countries and dispatched to poor ones.

Because Blessed couldn't afford sunglasses, he wrapped a litham across his face, squinting through slits in the cloth. Dust grated in his eyes and gritted between his teeth. It itched in every crevice of his skin, rasped in his throat, and stung his nostrils until they bled.

Rocking and jostling as if on camelback, they drove from first light until dusk, then stopped and cooked meals over camel-dung fires. The sealed road ran through towns inhabited by people of their tribe who sold them food and water and offered advice about conditions ahead. Then gradually the asphalt gave out, and the towns gave out too. From crumbling irrigation ditches, dead palms stuck out of scalded ground like blackened matchsticks. A great fire appeared to have ravished the land, and the few palms that survived had plastic bags fluttering from their fronds. They blew everywhere, these bags, reminding Blessed of the strips of torn cloth that Believers scribbled prayers on and tied to tree limbs.

They plunged through the reg, a fathomless expanse of heat mirages and scorched rocks. The bleached bones of animals sketched arabesques on the sand, and as the truck drummed past them, scavenging birds lifted off the skeletons, then resettled like ashes. Cairns of stones marked the tombs of dead migrants. These too attracted birds of prey and packs of wild dogs that scrabbled to dig up the bodies.

When they reached the border where their country ended and another started, soldiers in mismatched uniforms armed with automatic weapons ordered the truck to stop and the passengers to climb down. They demanded money and called it a tax.

Some passengers pleaded poverty, and the soldiers frisked them, roughed them up, and robbed them. The women resisted being touched, and a few men fought to protect them. But the soldiers beat them with rifle butts and stripped the women naked. Herded at gunpoint to the far side of the truck, the male passengers couldn't see what happened, but they heard it. They heard it and could do nothing. For miles around, the desert rang with the screams of women. Cursing his powerlessness, Blessed cowered with the other men.

After they bandaged themselves, the women climbed back on the truck, and the trek north resumed. No one spoke. The men didn't express sympathy, and the women didn't expect it. They had made up their minds months, even years, ago. They had hoarded up money and strength and hope, and nothing short of death would stop them.

They traveled now at night to hide from soldiers and from

thieves pretending to be soldiers. They slept in the dunes, where the sun's heat was horrible during the day, then set off after dark, when the cold was worse. Insects added to their afflictions, swarming into their mouths and eyes. Everywhere that Blessed scratched, his skin became infected. Still, five times a day, he faithfully pressed his forehead to the ground and repeated the same sura: "Well have you deserved this doom. Too well have you deserved it." He accepted his suffering as penance for not protecting the women.

In a sector of the Sahara where Polisario rebels had skirmished for decades against the Moroccans, an enormous berm of sand separated the pacified area from the free-fire zone. The berm bristled with land mines. To escape them, the driver abandoned the road, labored up mountainous dunes, and thundered down the far side, knocking everybody together on a nightmare roller-coaster ride.

One day it sounded as if they were crunching across a field of shattered glass. The driver paused in a fossil bed of petrified starfish and clamshells. Ignoring the threat of mines, they all climbed down and giddily scooped up sand dollars, as if they had discovered real treasure.

In Morocco, the road improved, and they could have sped through Marrakech and Fez to the coast. But they stayed to the east side of the Atlas range, where cedar stumps had washed down during flash floods, scattering the bed of the Dadès River with half-human shapes.

Casbahs built of hand-molded mud lined the valley, and for the first time in weeks, they drank water that was cold and sweet and ate bread that was fresh-baked. The road passed between braided palm fronds that kept the pavement clear of blowing sand. Farther on, in the Rif, barbed wire replaced these fragile fences. Farmers here grew kif, and armed smugglers in SUVs with tinted windows guarded the crop while women in brilliantly colored headwraps harvested the weed.

In a delirium of exhaustion, Blessed reached the Mediterranean, where they were supposed to be met by a man with a boat. Neither the man nor the boat was there. The truck driver dumped them in a cove and instructed them to wait. Too tired to protest, they bedded down on seaweed and kelp, half hopeful, half in despair. For fear they would be spotted by sea patrols, they built no fire and shivered through the night.

The next day, a different truck arrived, carrying a deflated rubber dinghy on its flatbed. They were ordered to hoist it onto the beach and pump its pontoons full with a foot pedal. Meanwhile, the boat's owner stood smoking and watching the Zodiac inflate and take shape. Then he pieced together a pair of plastic oars and snapped them into the oarlocks. From the cab of his truck, he fetched an outboard engine and bolted it to the stern of the dinghy. People grumbled that the boat wasn't big enough or seaworthy. But the man swore it was the right size and that the outboard had the power to cross the Straits of Gibraltar.

In the falling darkness, Blessed spent an hour praying. He didn't know how to swim. He had never been in a boat before and had trouble buckling on his flimsy life jacket. His hands shook, and his eyes refused to focus. It had paralyzed him with fear to think of dying in the desert, mummified by arid air. He decided it was worse to disappear into the ocean depths, leaving nothing of himself to be buried.

At dusk they dragged the dinghy off the beach, and while the boat owner manned the tiller, they walked it into the shockingly cold water. Inch by inch, the ocean swallowed their legs. When it was hip deep, they clambered over the pontoons, clutching their sopping bags, tangled together as hopelessly as they had been on the truck. As each passenger boarded, the Zodiac sank lower like a garbage scow.

The outboard engine coughed, cleared its throat, then roared to life but never gained any great speed. Although the sea looked calm, strong currents through the Straits of Gibraltar swung them sideways. Nothing the boatman did could hold them steady.

Blessed heard other engines, inhaled diesel fumes, and ducked rooster tails of spray. High-powered boats, all headed for Spain, threatened to swamp the dinghy. Worse, there were cruise ships as tall as apartment towers and oil tankers, a mile long, trailing whirlpools of debris and tempests of seagulls. Drones swarmed the sky, tracking drug runners and sex traffickers. They ignored the boat of refugees. One small floundering Zodiac didn't interest the police.

When the dinghy started to ship water, they had nothing to bail with except their hands. The engine quit, and passengers panicked, shouting and shoving. A woman tumbled overboard, and the boatman refused to circle back and save her. A man, maybe her husband, flung the boatman into the sea. But then no one knew how to steer the Zodiac or to restart the engine.

Rudderless, they wallowed in the swells behind the cruise ships. The tiller slapped uselessly back and forth. Blessed grabbed an oar and tried to row. But people desperate to save themselves scrambled over him. He didn't mean to hurt them. He only meant to protect himself. But lashing out with the oar, he heard and felt their bones crack.

Passengers fought back, and he was pushed overboard with the defective life jacket yoked around his neck. Flipping onto his back, he found that the tide would keep him afloat if he lay still. He gasped for air and spat out salt water. His eyes filled with stars, as drowning men and women made waves that carried him safely away.

When his feet touched bottom, he stumbled up onto the shore, where a volunteer rescue squad wrapped survivors in silver foil like fish packaged for market. They gestured for Blessed to lie down beside the bodies, some dead, some barely alive, lined up like macabre sunbathers on the beach. He shrugged off the foil cape, dashed to a seawall, and vaulted into the night.

He hiked next to a highway, hiding in the underbrush. He walked all night, away from the coast. At daybreak, he dropped in his tracks, covering himself with weeds. After a couple hours of sleep, he woke and spotted a road sign in Spanish and Arabic that indicated the route to Granada. He accepted this as Allah's will urging him to press on.

He stole fruit from an orange orchard which relieved his thirst but did little for his hunger. He hitched a ride on a produce truck, and in exchange for his help unpacking crates, the driver paid him with bottled water and bread.

Whether on foot or on a truck, Blessed felt seasick, as if he were still aboard the rubber boat, deafened by the screams of terrified men and women. Whatever part of him hadn't died in the Sahara, he thought, had been killed at sea. This was the afterlife. Heaven or hell, he couldn't say which. His head wasn't huge enough to hold all the questions he had.

In Granada, after the incalculable distance he had traveled, it seemed he was back where he had started—back in the Islamic world. The Alhambra reminded him of the mud casbahs in the Draa Valley, their perfection magnified a hundred times, too beautiful to be lived in or even entered by the likes of Blessed. When he dared to approach it, he discovered that it cost money to visit the Alhambra—far more than he earned begging outside the Italian *gelateria.* Then, through the mercy of Allah, the All-Powerful and Compassionate, Paul gave him a few euros, a sort of job, and a place to sleep. Although Blessed had been taught to distrust white people, he also knew to kiss the hand he could not cut off.

• • •

Waking on his pallet in the supply closet, he whispered a morning sura: "I swear by this city (and you yourself are a resident of this city) by the Begetter and all whom He begat: We created man to try him with afflictions." Patsy fixed him a breakfast of black coffee, a day-old *barra de pan*, and a drizzle of honey in a dish. He believed that gifts make slaves just as whips make dogs, but he thanked her and ate hastily, as if to disguise from himself what he was doing.

Patsy's skin was pale chocolate, but she was as African as Blessed. She told him she had been trafficked from Cape Verde, and she spoke some Arabic and an island Creole that he could, with difficulty, follow.

After eating, Blessed went to work in the courtyard. During the skull-cracking heat of summer, it had made sense to start early in its tree shade. Now, in autumn, he kept the same schedule, although it was cool enough for him to need a sweater. He relished being alone, imagining he was minding land that belonged to him.

Paul seldom bothered counting the baskets of prunes and pears and strawberries that Blessed picked. Nor did he object to how much fruit Blessed ate. Patsy accused Paul of being softhearted and wasteful, and Blessed agreed. There were dozens of repairs that could have improved the *carmen*. But Blessed didn't feel confident to mention them. Though he understood almost everything Paul said, he turned tongue-tied every time he tried to speak English.

One day, a guest spotted a snake in the strawberry patch. Paul instructed Blessed to find it and kill it before a resident was bitten or, just as bad, got scared and left the *carmen*. Blessed tried to convince him that the snake wasn't a danger to people. It preyed on field mice and rats. But the right words slipped away, much like the garden snake slithered through the strawberry plants, barely disturbing them.

Eventually Blessed trapped it against a wall and hacked off its head with a shovel. When Blessed picked it up, the snake tightened around his fingers, and blood spurted from its neck. Down on the ground, the snake's severed head might have been the tip of an arrow, motionless except for its flickering tongue. Blessed lacked the words to describe how he felt—not much different from witnessing a man's decapitation.

Some days when he cleaned Paul's office, he found the computer online, its lid raised. Blessed didn't dare type an email to his family. Still, he risked logging onto Dibaq for the Arab-language news, which often broadcast videos of executions—blasphemers crucified, adulterers stoned to death, nonbelievers garroted.

One film clip lodged in his mind like a scorpion's stinger. A white man in an orange jumpsuit knelt next to a tall figure in black robes who glared through the eyeholes of what looked like a woman's niqab. The man in black waved a butcher knife and spoke with an accent that Blessed didn't realize was British. The Arabic crawl at the bottom of the screen identified the kneeling man as an infidel, a soldier in the Great Satan's crusade against the caliphate. He had been condemned to death because the United States refused to negotiate an exchange of prisoners.

Granted permission to speak, the condemned man, to Blessed's amazement, didn't plead for mercy. Nor did he scream in fear or curse his executioner. Weirdly calm—was he drugged?—he declared that he had converted to Islam and repented his sins.

This made no difference to the man with the butcher knife. He seized the American by the hair, yanked back his head, and decapitated him as easily as Blessed had beheaded the harmless snake. The camera closed in on the dying man's eyes as they glazed over. Then it cut to the blood that frothed from his throat, saturating the orange jumpsuit. The British executioner kept speaking, but Blessed didn't check the crawl for a translation. He couldn't take his eyes off the human head, so small and insignificant in the sand.

On later visits to Paul's office, Blessed found what he thought was the same video on other Arab websites. He watched the execution many times before it dawned on him that while the masked man with the knife was always the same, the condemned man changed. The British executioner dispatched each captive as coldly as he would a chicken.

As the dead men bled out, imams sometimes debated the concept of *takfir.* Was terrorism morally justified? Was it permissible to commit murder, to slaughter innocent souls, in defense of the faith? Some scholars argued that killing was a sin, forbidden in all cases by the Koran. Others spoke in favor of necessary evil, of sin committed to achieve a greater good—like Paul ordering Blessed to kill the snake to keep his paying guests happy.

Queasy, Blessed couldn't stop thinking about the white men who had been beheaded. Because they claimed to have converted to Islam, didn't they qualify as martyrs? Shouldn't their souls, as the Prophet promised, "reside in green birds, nesting in lanterns hung from the throne of the Almighty, roaming freely to eat the fruits of Paradise"? It was another question he felt inadequate to answer.

Finishing his outside chores, Blessed moved indoors. This part of his job was much less to his liking. Cleaning bathrooms was women's work. Still, he scrubbed the toilets and bathtubs until they gleamed and mopped the floors so that they smelled of sweet oils.

The artist lady's suite was aromatic of perfume, shampoo, and body creams. Over the shower rod dangled sherbet-colored underpants and black mesh brassieres. Blessed fought the temptation to touch them and didn't succeed. The texture of the material between his fingertips was as silky soft as a woman's skin.

Late at night on his pallet, he remembered that softness and the woman's smells as he lay rigid, mumbling from the Book, "I seek refuge from the mischief of the slinking prompter who whispers in the hearts of men." Yet he couldn't quit touching himself any more than he could stop caressing the bras and panties.

The walls of Simone's studio were muraled with watercolors that struck Blessed like a mallet to the forehead, the sort of swift blow he had dealt farm animals before slitting their throats. Breathless, he obsessed over the pictures, petrified that he would be found out.

Because he had noticed no strange men entering the *carmen*, he concluded that these images sprang straight from the artist lady's brain. Boys sprawled naked in bed, just as he lay on his pallet at night, clutching his *zeb*. On an easel, a painting showed what Blessed assumed was the artist lady's own body. Between unimaginable white thighs, a *kus* spread like a fig. He had seen very few naked women, none during daylight. Girls in his village had all been cut as children, the flesh between their legs reduced to scar tissue. But the body on the easel had been *halawa* waxed, exposing complicated creases and furrows, like a mouth with lips inside lips and the tiniest tip of a tongue.

Blessed collected his mop and bucket, his broom and dustpan, and after storing them in the closet, he tried to think. Then he tried not to think. But he couldn't scrub the images from his mind. Climbing the stairs to Paul's office, he declared that he could no longer clean the artist lady's room. If that meant he was fired, he accepted his fate.

Paul invited him to sit down and explain. This was a liberty Blessed was reluctant to permit himself. When Paul insisted, Blessed perched on a chair and glanced at the computer on the desk, half expecting to witness another execution. But the screen saver showed a young white boy on a beach beside a violently blue sea. It was an instant before it registered on him that the boy was his boss as a child.

"Tell me," Paul urged him.

"Allah, praise be his name," Blessed began in Arabic before switching to a hodgepodge of Spanish and English to express that Allah had created man and woman from clots of blood. Only He could make a human body. No one else, not the artist lady. All such images were haram.

Paul said he understood and promised to speak to Simone. "Don't worry. This will work out," Paul assured him.

"Inshallah."

CHAPTER III

The dining room at the residence extended off the kitchen, with a rough-hewn wooden table and cane-bottom chairs for a dozen guests. Its wall display of copper pots and pans, ceramic jars and platters, gave it the homey feel of a country hacienda. Because of the table's proximity to the stove, Patsy could save steps and simply plunk down a breakfast of tortillas, bread, and coffee in cups the size of cereal bowls. The coziest spot in the *carmen*, the kitchen was a constant temptation for guests to linger, especially on winter mornings.

Today the ambient-sound guy had departed early with his dead cat to record the town's static pulse. Paul and Simone sat across from each other, while Patsy, in a great charade of busyness, cleared dirty dishes from the table. A tiny, tense-muscled woman with brassy blond hair, she never bothered to conceal her nosiness—nor her bossiness—about Paul's private life. While she scrutinized him and the new guest, he asked Simone in a subdued voice to take a walk with him.

"I haven't been to the Alhambra yet," Simone said.

"That's a hassle. You have to buy tickets in advance and make a reservation."

"I'll book online, and we can go this afternoon."

"I've maxed out on the Alhambra," he admitted. "It hasn't been the same for me since I heard that the Kufic calligraphy on the walls repeats a single phrase nine thousand times: 'Only Allah is victorious.'"

"What a load of world-weary BS."

Patsy followed their conversation like a tennis match, her head swiveling back and forth.

"What I'm weary of," Paul said, "is all these tourists jabbing each other with selfie sticks. They suck the soul out of the place."

"Sounds to me," Simone taunted, "like you're the one whose soul has been sucked away."

"One hundred percent correct."

"And now that you've lost your capacity for wonder, you're willing to blow off a World Heritage Site."

"I'm not blowing off anything. I'd just rather show you the real Granada."

"Okay, let me change."

"I'll wait for you out front," he said, eager to escape Patsy's surveillance.

Simone returned wearing black Nike running shoes and a black sweater loose around her shoulders. "Do I look like a nun? Or an aging widow?"

"You look fine," he said.

In fact, she looked terrific. As they stepped out of the shadow of the *carmen*, the sharp, apple-scented light deepened the luster of her hair, its gold streaks fluttering in autumn wind. At Mirador San Nicolas, he watched while she snapped the obligatory cell-phone shot of the Alhambra across the valley. Dogs frolicked around her feet while a guitarist picked out the opening bars of *Concierto de Aranjuez* and a tattooed girl in copper earrings passed a tambourine for tips. In the summer's blowtorch heat, this plaza had been abandoned. Six weeks from now, icy rain would empty it again. For the moment, it was a perfect temperature, a perfect place to admire the view.

Just around the corner, at a discreet distance from a Catholic church, the Mezquita de Granada, the first mosque in the city since the Reconquista, had opened in 2003. With emotions still raw after 9-11, there had been public protests during its construction. Perhaps that was why the architect had muted the building's Islamic motifs.

"Is this another site on your bucket shit list?" Simone asked.

"Not at all. Knock yourself out. Look around as long as you like."

After a short stroll through the mosque's courtyard and inner compound, she came back laughing. "I love the satellite dish and the coffee machine. They remind me of the snack bar at Auschwitz."

"You're joking."

"No joke. I've been there. Done that. No T-shirt, though."

On Cuesta del Chapiz, they swung down against the steep, grinding uphill traffic.

"How's the work coming?" Paul asked. "Anything you need?"

"Time and quiet are all I need."

"That we can provide. As for other stuff, I realize you've been at better-equipped residencies. I apologize for our shortcomings."

"No apologies necessary."

"Okay, I won't apologize, and I won't give in to my curiosity about why you chose the *carmen*. But I need to explain that there are certain eccentricities we have to respect and work around."

Just then a German family—sun-pinkened *Vater, Mutter, und zwei Kinder* in matching lederhosen—lumbered by. "Is that the sort of eccentricity you mean?"

He attempted to mimic her good-natured tone. He didn't want to sound like some raving woke scold.

"Blessed complained to me yesterday," he said. "Cleaning your studio, he saw your work and blew a fuse."

"No kidding? What did he like best? The watercolors or the oil painting?" Her voice was thick with sarcasm.

"For Muslims, the human figure is haram."

"Help me out here."

"Haram means forbidden. The Koran insists that only Allah can create men and women. Islamic artists, you've probably noticed, stick to abstractions."

"Actually, I'd like to paint Blessed. He's so black he's almost blue, like some of the models in Mapplethorpe's photographs."

They crossed the Darro on Puente Rey Chico and advanced with the river crackling over its bed on their left. Paul wasn't aware of where they were headed until it was too late. Whenever possible, he avoided this spot.

"It's no joke. Blessed threatens to quit rather than be exposed to your art."

"So his soul is in my hands," she drawled.

"No, I'm in your hands. It's impossible to find help as honest and dependable as Blessed. I'd hate to lose him. And I hate to imagine what'll happen to him if he winds up out on the street."

"I don't suppose he confessed he's been grubbing around in my bras and underpants?"

"He didn't mention that, just that he's upset by the pictures."

"To be honest with you, Pablo . . ." Where did that come from? Had she heard Patsy use his nickname? "I didn't become an artist to please Muslim boys." A steel thread insinuated itself into her irony.

"Blessed's a man. A good one. I promised him we'd sort this out."

"What do you suggest? Should I turn my work to the wall?"

Her attitude rankled him. It had, in fact, crossed his mind to suggest that she move her art out of sight for a short time each day. Instead, he asked, "What if Patsy cleaned your room?"

"Fine. Maybe she'll pose for me."

"That's a thought. I can't wait to hear her reaction."

"What about you?"

"I'm not one to pull rank, but I don't clean rooms."

"I mean what about modeling for me?"

He assumed she wasn't serious; he assumed they were back to bantering. "That'd be a boundary offense. A violation of the director-guest relationship."

"Don't play holier-than-thou. Not with your reputation—every aspiring female artist's heartthrob."

"You've got me confused with another guy." He refused to take the bait and fish for what she'd heard and from whom. "You damn well never heard of me posing in the nude. Or dressed, for that matter. I maintain my professional distance."

"You're funny. You know that?" she said. "Behind your beard, you look pensive and severe, like Vincent van Gogh. But you're Van Gogh with a good sense of humor."

From the path where they walked, they could glance up at the Generalife with its clean white walls like an ocean liner's. Nearer to them, a purple rope swagged through the shrubbery, as if marking off first-class cabins. "How do you suppose that got there?" Simone asked.

"Probably a flash flood."

"The river gets that deep?" Without waiting for an answer, Simone kicked at a deflated inner tube on the bank. "Doesn't it remind you of one of Salvador Dali's deliquescing clocks?"

Paul wouldn't admit what it reminded him of. As a kid, he used to jog here. One afternoon, a woman soaked with sweat and hysteria had clutched him by the shoulders and screamed that her little boy had fallen into the Darro and was drowning. "Save him," she begged.

Muddied by recent storms, the river was sick-green and opaque. Paul doubted that its indolent current could drag even a small child under. But the woman insisted, "He's down there," and pushed him toward the water.

He kicked off his shoes and tiptoed into the stream up to his ankles. The next step took him in over his knees. Then a trapdoor seemed to open under his feet, and he sank over his head, choking on silt. A storm had gouged out a deep hole. Its sides were spiked with tree roots, like a fish trap. He struggled hard to break free and crawl ashore.

He told the woman he didn't believe her son was down there. Still, he urged her to run to a phone and call the rescue squad. He swore he'd continue searching. But after she left, he crouched on the riverbank, paralyzed. A bead of panic bubbled in his chest, slowly swelling in size, overwhelming his whole body, stealing all his strength. Only his mind moved, fumbling to persuade him that the woman was delusional. She didn't have a son. Nobody had slipped into the river.

He didn't fear drowning. He was a good swimmer. What he feared was that a dead body had snagged in the underwater debris. He desperately didn't want to touch it, to pull a corpse out of the Darro and kiss its cold lips, attempting mouth-to-mouth respiration.

With Paul still hunched on the shore, the rescue squad arrived and unspooled a hose attached to a gas-powered pump. In minutes, it suctioned the little boy up from the river, stiff and blue as a gigged frog, his face slimed with leaves. Paul watched them drag him ashore. A man slammed the heels of his hands into the boy's chest. There was an audible cracking of ribs. The rescue squad tried everything—oxygen from a tank, more chest pounding, more mouth-to-mouth. Nothing worked.

They stretchered the kid into an ambulance and, with the sobbing mother riding along, sped off as if some miracle might happen at the hospital. A member of the rescue squad stayed behind to collect the equipment and assured Paul that he had done all he could. He called Paul a hero. Paul knew better. Ever since that day, the bead of panic had stewed inside him, waiting for the right circumstances—or the wrong ones—to well up again and overcome him. Where most people lived in fear of death, Paul Stewart dreaded being tested and found wanting once more. He had never told this to anyone, and his only consolation was that his father had died without knowing any of it.

• • •

Simone and he hit a dead end at the gate to Carmen de la Fuente and retraced their steps. "What do you think of my work?" Simone asked.

"Are you really interested in my opinion?"

"I wouldn't ask otherwise."

"What can I say that critics haven't already written?"

"Forget the art-speak and tell me what you feel."

"Okay, I'm fascinated. And confused. I can't figure out how it fits in with #MeToo."

"It's got nothing to do with #MeToo. I'm not part of any movement. Unless it's the classical tradition," she added half facetiously. "The proper study of man being man—and of course woman."

As she punctuated these points with her hands, he noticed that her fingernails were bitten off and ragged, her palms rough from turpentine and paint remover.

"Are you claiming you don't mean to shock?" he asked.

"These days, it takes more than what I do to shock people. Have you seen the sexts junior high students send each other? I just want to wake people up and force them to look with new eyes. I side with Magritte: 'Everything we see hides another thing. We always want to see what's behind what we see.'"

"I don't buy that you don't have a deeper agenda."

"If I have one, it's to pay the same attention to female genitals as artists have historically paid to men's. It's to privilege women with agency. To prove that females aren't mere receptacles."

This sounded to Paul like something recycled from past interviews. He changed the subject. "Do you work from models or the imagination?"

"I admire artists who can stay in their studios and invent a whole world. I'm not one of them. I have to paint from real life, from what I find on my computer."

"And that's real life?" he asked.

"It's as real as it gets. Chat Random hooks me up with hundreds of people. Africans, Asians, Eastern Europeans, all eager to pose. Most of them are already naked when I log on."

"Do they expect to be paid?"

"That's not part of the deal."

"Do they expect you to be naked?"

"Some do. But I make it clear that I'm there to do art, nothing else."

"Don't any of them have their own demands?"

"If they do, I push a button and they disappear. That's the beauty of the computer. Compared to the problems with professional studio models, it's a breeze."

"What do they get out of it?"

"You'd have to ask them. Maybe they're lonely. Maybe they're exhibitionists. For me, online anonymity is a great advantage. People are less inhibited. Their bodies aren't airbrushed or aerobicized. Some of them still have lines where their underwear was. No matter where I am, I have subjects to paint."

"Subjects? You talk about them like objects."

"Don't put words in my mouth." She gave him a friendly shoulder bump.

"How do you think they feel?"

"I don't have a clue. There's no personal involvement. What

I love is the light on Chat Random. You get all these strange streaks and color bleeds. When there are faults in the connection, skin has an iridescent sheen."

They paused under trees pungent with pine resin and eucalyptus bark. Through the slatted light between branches, the last few butterflies of the season fell like musical notes on a staff. "I'm surprised you'd leave the States, where the Wi-Fi is dependable," he said.

"I've wanted to visit Spain. I once had a boyfriend who was a fanatic for Lorca," she said. "He quoted this line about a woman drinking cool water from a man's lips. In the middle of the night, when I was thirsty, he'd bring me water in his mouth."

"And you drank it? I'd say you were both hopeless romantics."

She broke into a grin. "Is it romance or Lorca you don't like?"

"Lorca's great. The family maid used to quote him. 'In Spain the dead are more alive than the dead in any other country.' He was assassinated not far from here."

"That's not something my boyfriend mentioned. Anyway, I recently saw a performance of *Yerma*, and the next thing you know, I sublet my apartment and caught a plane to Granada."

"My father was interested in Lorca," Paul said. "That's how he met my mother. Back in the '70s, he had a Fulbright here to write a book about him."

"I'd love to read it."

"He never wrote it. He had this habit of signing contracts, then never delivering books. When publishers threatened legal action, he'd bug out for the islands."

"Sounds like a fascinating guy."

"Plenty of women agreed with you."

"But not your mother, I'm guessing."

"No, they didn't last long."

"And what was your relationship with him like?"

"That's a story for another day. For a long, rainy day."

"I look forward to it. At least I know now how you ended up in Granada."

"I didn't *end up*. It's where I started. For a time, I traveled back and forth to the States, never able to make up my mind."

"Now you've made it up for good?"

"Who knows about good?"

"Philosophers and priests and people who have their shit together, they know about good."

"Have you met many of them?"

"No, but I'm always on the lookout."

They recrossed the river on a bridge where a fisherman had discarded a starburst of scales on the railing. "Let me buy you lunch," Simone said

"I have to head back and talk Patsy into cleaning your room."

"Sorry to cause trouble."

"No trouble," he told her, although all signs suggested that Simone *was* big trouble and he should be on guard.

"I'll explore on my own." She offered him her hard-worked hand. "This has been fun. You don't meet many men who like to talk and are willing to listen."

Hiking to the *carmen*, Paul mulled over Simone's comment. Laconic men, the strong, silent type, starting with his father, had always been the standard he measured himself against. Although plenty of women claimed to appreciate good conversation, he thought soaking up and squeezing out words called to mind nothing better than a soft, damp sponge.

• • •

Patsy was at the kitchen stove, stirring a pot of lentil stew—another sign that the season had changed. In summer, she fixed batches of gazpacho, which guests drank by the gallon like Gatorade. Afraid that Blessed might overhear them from the storage space, Paul motioned for Patsy to step outside.

"You've got a visitor," she told him.

Perched on the lip of the fountain in the garden, an immense fat man gazed down at the drift of koi. He wore an embroidered white shirt, a guayabera, that flapped loose at his waist.

"Who is he?" Paul asked.

"An American. He claims he's from the embassy in Madrid."

They were speaking Spanish. Patsy had an accent; Paul was thoroughly fluent in the language. But to irritate him, she sometimes threw in a few phrases of Cabo Verdean Creole.

"What does he want?"

"I'll bet he'll tell you if you ask," she said with a borderline insolence that was becoming habitual.

"I'll do that. First, I need a favor. Blessed is offended by the lady artist's paintings and refuses to clean her room. Will you take over that job?"

She snorted in derision.

"I'll make it up to you," he said.

"Make it up how?"

"With money."

"Good. I've seen her paintings. You'll have to pay me double to put up with those *caralhos* and that giant *cona*."

"She'll probably invite you to pose for her."

"I'm not the type to parade around flaunting my private parts."

"Okay, keep your clothes on and just clean her room."

Paul strolled over to the fountain where the fat man was lighting a cigarette. Smoke licked up over his meaty face, and ashes dribbled down his front. He didn't resemble any diplomat Paul had ever seen.

"We have a rule against smoking," Paul said.

"Even out in the garden?"

"Even here. The residents insist on it."

"Okay, where can I smoke while we talk?" he asked, not unpleasantly.

Just as pleasantly, Paul told him there was a plaza in front of the *carmen*.

"I'm Bill Spann. Can I call you Pablo?"

There it was again. Did some website carry his name in Spanish? "Paul will do fine," he said.

When they shook hands, Spann's palm was soft and damp. Although he appeared to be a pudge ball, he moved with surprising nimbleness, like a pulling guard ready to knock a linebacker on his butt. As they passed through the *carmen*, he performed a trick Paul hadn't seen since college: he tipped the cigarette into his mouth on his tongue and didn't exhale until they were outside.

From Huerta de Carlos, steps led down to a deserted playground. Paul seldom saw kids here. The metal swings and slide were scalding hot in summer and glacially cold in winter. On a wall behind the jungle gym, graffiti artists had sprayed exotic signs and symbols and a couple of lines in English that Paul assumed had been scribbled by a previous resident: "Truth is a book." "Fewer cowboys. More Apaches."

Part of the playground was given over to exercise equipment for adults. Bill Spann straddled a stationary bike. Along with pedals, it had handlebars that he rowed back and forth. "I need to get into shape, lose some weight."

When his cigarette burned down to a nub, Spann spat it out and lit another. "If I were you, I'd be out here every day."

"Running the residency is more than enough exercise."

"How many rooms you got?" Spann resumed pumping the stationary bike at high speed.

"Patsy said you were from the US Embassy. I didn't realize you were looking for a room."

"Not for myself. For somebody else. First, I need a little background info. How many rooms are occupied at the moment?"

"Two. Look, Mr. Spann, I've dealt with cultural officials at the embassy. I don't remember meeting you. Are you new in Madrid?"

He chuckled. "No, I'm middle-aged in Madrid, and I'm not cultural. Let's leave it that I'm political."

"We steer clear of politics. We stick to the arts. Our mission—"

"Yeah, I read your mission statement online, and I think we may have a match. You see, on the political side, we have a cultural situation. What I gather—beg your pardon if I'm off base—you don't just accept Americans. You welcome foreigners."

"We actively seek diversity."

"Bravo. I noticed you're incorporated in Delaware as a not-for-profit. And you're squared away with the Spanish authorities. That's all good."

Spann had started to stream sweat. Paul was beginning to feel clammy himself. Discussions of the *carmen*'s tax status always had that effect on him.

"The cook and the Black houseboy," Spann said, "do they have papers?"

"What's the US Embassy's interest in that?"

"Hey, don't get touchy. Just tell me where the cook comes from?"

"Cape Verde. She's got a Portuguese passport and EU citizenship."

"And the houseboy?"

"I have no idea."

A deep frown gouged lines in Spann's plump cheeks. "You never asked?"

"Don't ask, don't tell. Isn't that US policy?"

"Yeah, for gays in the military. Not for potential terrorists."

Paul's stomach dropped. "Is there something about Blessed I don't know?"

"That's the point. These days, the world we live in, you never know. You'd be smart to ask more questions." Spann quit pedaling and rowing, and the wheels and handlebars spun on their own. Spann waited until they slowed to a stop before he said, "There's an Algerian university professor that interests us. He's a writer, a sort of Salman Rushdie. We think your place would be perfect to stash him while he finishes his book. He taught in Tlemcen, which he tells us is a sister city to Granada. Same architecture, same cultural history. This would feel like home to him."

"What's his name?" Paul asked.

"Tahar Mahmoud. He's done scholarly stuff and articles for French-language newspapers and literary magazines. Now, what I gather, he's switching gears and writing a novel, retelling a story by Camus from an Arab's point of view. Something about terrorism being the contemporary plague."

"There's already a book like that," Paul said, "based on Albert Camus's *The Stranger.*" When he mentioned *The Meursault Investigation* by Kamel Daoud, Spann didn't react.

"It caused a huge stink," Paul went on. "Muslims in Algeria were enraged. Imams declared a fatwa against Daoud for insulting Islam. They sentenced him to death."

Spann folded his arms across his big belly, which was as pink as a boiled ham under his shirt. "Sounds like what Tahar went through. His university students and administrators accused him of blasphemy and said he should be executed. Some group kidnapped him and tortured him. We figure he's worth helping."

Spann's expression of sympathy sat uneasily with the menace his size projected. He reminded Paul of a barroom bouncer—the kind who behaves benevolently right up until he starts breaking bones. "As an American, I'm sure you're aware of our history of humanitarian aid."

"Maybe I've been out of the country too long."

Spann grinned, the sort of smile that on a baby might be a symptom of gas pains. "Well, I admit we have more than charity in mind. We want to hide Mr. Mahmoud in a safe house while we debrief him."

"Tell him to submit his résumé and a description of his project, and we'll evaluate it."

Spann dismounted from the exercise bike and dealt his balls a brisk shake. "Let's not bullshit each other, Pablo. I don't buy that you abide by HEW guidelines and conduct peer reviews. I bet you operate out of your hip pocket."

Spann waddled over to the children's part of the playground and flopped onto a swing.

Struggling to separate the strands of the conversation—they felt braided together as tightly as a noose—Paul weighed the damage he might do himself if he refused to get involved. The residency skirted so many regulations and was so financially precarious, it would take very little to nudge it over the edge.

Then it came to him that this might have some crazy connection to his father. Maybe US intelligence retained a file on Peter Stewart and figured that his son would gladly serve as an asset.

Paul lowered himself onto the swing beside Spann. The chains squeaked. "I'm afraid you're under a false impression about me."

"We don't deal in impressions," Spann said. "We deal in facts."

"That's what confuses me. What 'facts' brought you here?"

"That's not information I can share. What I can tell you is we plan to handle this strictly off the books. We'll transport Mahmoud to Granada by means you don't need to worry about, and while he's here, we'll monitor him and check out his story about his time in prison. He's asking for asylum and a university job in the States. To get that, he needs to have something valuable to trade."

"How long would he be here?"

"Depends."

"On what?"

"On how much he knows about ISIS and AQIM. How many names and faces he can add to the database. Then his book, when he's finished, we'll decide whether it's worth translating into different languages."

"The US is in the publishing business?"

"Ever since the Cold War, we've been a major player. When *Doctor Zhivago* was smuggled out of Russia, we had it translated into a slew of languages and distributed around the globe. Great publicity for the USA, not so much for Moscow."

"But why Spain? Why not hide this guy in France?"

"That's the first place they'd hunt for him."

"What if they track him here?"

"They won't. The transfer to Granada will be airtight. Your place has bars on the windows and a front door that could stop a tank. You're miles off the grid. I had hell's own trouble locating you with GPS."

"Still, there's a risk."

"No risk compared to what we'll pay you to clear out the other rooms and let Mahmoud move in."

"Hold on," Paul protested. "I can't turn away business and shut down the residency."

"How many people do you have here now?"

"I told you—two."

Spann flashed his oleaginous grin. "So folks aren't exactly

busting a gut to get in, are they? You're teetering on the brink, Pablo. This is your chance to turn things around."

The embassy must have accessed his tax returns. After a quick mental calculation, Paul said, "I'd need ten thousand a month, with five months guaranteed."

"Done." Spann clapped a hand on Paul's knee.

"Not yet. One guest, an American composer, is scheduled to leave at the end of the week. But an artist just got here, and she paid in advance. She's an important painter. I can't evict her."

"An American?"

"Yes."

"Okay, she and the Portuguese cook can stay. But it's adios to the Black houseboy."

"He does all the work."

"And I bet you pay him peanuts."

This hit uncomfortably close to home. "It's not a matter of money," Paul said. "He's a good man."

"He's a Muslim. Probably an Arabic speaker."

"He barely speaks at all."

"He might have read about Mahmoud online."

"I don't think Blessed's literate. I've never noticed him reading."

"If he stays, that's a deal-breaker."

They fell quiet, and there was only the creaking of the swing and the evening's first guitar chords from the plaza. Much as he hated to cut Blessed loose, Paul couldn't afford to refuse the money.

"You love this Black guy so much," Spann said, "why not put him on vacation status? Throw him a few extra bucks to carry him over until he can move back in."

"I'll have to think it over."

"I'll give you till the end of the week."

Spann stood up and jiggled his balls again, as if reintroducing himself to an old friend. Paul stayed seated. "Did you choose me because of my father?" he asked.

"Say what?"

"My father, Peter Stewart. He worked for US intelligence. At least he claimed he did. My mother accused him of spying for the CIA."

"No shit." Spann chuckled. "When was this? Where?"

"Here in the early '70s during Franco's last years. Later he was a professor in Florida. Every so often he'd disappear and explain he was on assignment."

"Maybe he had a girlfriend."

"He had plenty of girlfriends. But he indicated he had ties to Langley. His bedroom bureau was full of handguns. Not standard equipment for a comp lit scholar."

"Sounds to me like a good American who believed in his right to bear arms."

Paul stood up, and the swing clipped the back of his knees. "That doesn't answer the question about my father."

"Relax, Pablo. Let me assure you we picked you because of your sterling character. That and the fact you have a house at the ass end of the world that's built like Fort Knox."

• • •

The tower was airless, oppressive, far too hot for an autumn night. Paul stripped to his underwear and stretched out on the single bed. When he shut his eyes, he heard his heartbeat and the clamor of the city around him. Fireworks, flamenco music, the rustle of palm fronds, the faint *plop!* of dates plunging to the ground in the garden. He struggled to understand the day's confounding events. No sooner had Blessed confronted him about Simone than Spann had given him an excuse to get rid of the houseboy. Why did he feel such guilt and disquiet over something so straightforward?

He climbed out of bed and opened the shutters. There was the scent of jasmine but not the slightest breeze. He lifted the lid on the computer and surfed. He wasn't in the mood to deal with his creditors or applications from aspiring artists. He Googled William Spann and confirmed that he was attached to the US Embassy in Madrid as an independent contractor.

Typing in "Tahar Mahmoud," Paul unearthed dozens of entries for a professor of philology in Tlemcen, the author of essays in French and Arabic on literary theory and current events. Paul skimmed them, then several readers' comments attacking Mahmoud for anti-Islamic secularism, religious heresy, seditious teaching, and failure to force his female students to wear hijabs. Imams judged that Mahmoud deserved the death penalty and promised his killer a martyr's reward—the loving embrace of virgins in paradise.

It was useless to Google Blessed. He was among the world's billions of "invisibles," too miserable to rate a mention online. Paul liked to believe that he sided with life's bottom dogs. Still, he would let Blessed go.

That was awful enough. To transform the *carmen* temporarily into a US black site ratcheted up his guilt—even though it was for causes he morally favored: rescuing a prisoner of conscience, providing a safe place for an author to complete a novel. Would he rather Tahar Mahmoud be rearrested and tortured again because of Paul's reluctance to help?

He couldn't shake the suspicion that the situation was linked to his father. A penny psychoanalyst might speculate that for Paul, everything was related to the man whose long absences had been only slightly less painful than his appalling presence. He recalled a school holiday in Florida, an evening at the dinner table with the young woman his father was living with at the moment. Peter Stewart was reading a book, *A Guide to Caribbean Fish.* As he ate, occasionally he declaimed passages aloud, as if lecturing students. "Listen to this. 'A remora, often called a suckerfish or a sharksucker, is one to three feet long and has a distinctive organ that allows it to create suction and attach itself to larger marine animals. The relationship between the remora and its host gives nothing to the host but provides transportation, protection and food for the remora. There is debate about the remora's diet. Is it leftover food from the host? Or the host's feces? Dissections have strongly suggested the remora is a feces eater.'"

His father snapped the guide shut. "Who does that sound like?"

Paul assumed his father saw him as a remora. Or was he referring to his ex-wife, who pestered him about late support payments? Probably he saw them both as shit-eating suckerfish.

The young woman at the table piped up, "I may be a remora, but you're a big ugly barracuda."

"At least barracudas don't feed on feces," his father shot back.

"No, they eat contaminated reef fish and turn toxic."

Peter Stewart flung out a hand, smacking her face. The print of his splayed fingers reddened her cheek as tears beaded her eyelashes.

Paul's eyes swam with tears too. He vowed he would never hit a woman—a promise that he still kept, although he was aware of wounding them in other ways.

• • •

Starlight allowed Paul to make out the rooftops of the Albaicín. Wildflowers and weeds had flourished on the tiles in summer. Now they had dried into fuzz, like the hair on an infant's skull. There was a word for that. There was a word for everything. He consulted an online dictionary and discovered "lanugo"—fine, downy hair. He was reminded of Simone Pierce's bare arms. Much as he regretted losing Blessed, he relished the idea of being alone with her. Alone except for the Algerian refugee.

CHAPTER IV

Paul came down to the kitchen early and brewed a pot of coffee and boiled milk. By the time Patsy arrived, he was on his second cup. Crabby at this hour, she snapped, "Are you the cook now? Am I just the janitor?"

"I'd be grateful if you'd fix me an omelet."

She placed her purse where she could keep an eye on it, unwound a scarf from her brassy hair, and shrugged a sweater from her shoulders. Under it, she wore an elasticized tube top that hugged her meager chest. "You look like a field worker in that denim shirt," she said. "How do you expect anyone to respect you as the jefe? You have no more ambition than an oyster."

He sighed. "What would I ever do without you to keep me in line?"

"I like to work in a dignified house. I don't want to be disgraced in my old age."

"You're no older than I am."

"But I have higher standards."

Blessed stepped out of the supply closet, lugging his belongings in a plastic bag labeled "Hypermarché." In his other hand, he held a pair of shoes with their heels pressed together. For a Muslim, shoe soles were dirty, impure, and he didn't care to offend anyone.

"What are you doing?" Paul asked.

"Leaving. Patsy tells me."

"I told him nothing except you asked me to clean the whore's room."

"Don't call her that," Paul said.

"Okay, the artist lady."

Paul thought he knew why Patsy was stroppier than usual. She and Blessed had been discussing their grievances. He asked her to fix an omelet for Blessed as well, motioned him to a chair at the table, and poured him a *café* con leche. Perhaps because it was a chilly morning, perhaps because his plastic bag couldn't contain everything he owned, Blessed wore several layers of clothing. The collars of a brown T-shirt, a black pullover, and a Franklin & Marshall sweatshirt sagged around his stringy neck. Despite his downcast expression, his cornrows, tufted with orange tips, danced merrily.

After Patsy served up their eggs, Paul told her he wanted privacy, and she left the kitchen. Blessed folded his omelet inside a slab of bread, improvising a *bric à l'oeuf* like those available in Little Morocco. While they ate, Paul spoke quietly, deliberately, spacing his words in Spanish. When Blessed seemed bewildered, he repeated himself in English, stressing how sorry he was, worrying about how much made it through to Blessed. Business was bad, he said. Too few paying guests. Maybe in a couple of months, things might be better, and he'd rehire Blessed. But for now . . . for now it wasn't possible to keep him on.

Blessed mumbled about the artist lady.

"It has nothing to do with her. It's a matter of money." Paul mentioned nothing about the Algerian writer or Spann.

"I work free. No money, just sleep and eat here."

"Not now," Paul said.

Blessed pushed the last of the food into his mouth with his callused hands. His fingers were nimble, the nails shrimp pink.

"I'll find you," Paul promised.

"How?"

"Granada isn't a big city. I'll find you."

"Where I live."

"Yes. Exactly."

Blessed murmured, "Where I live," a second time, and Paul realized it was a question that had no answer. He handed him a hundred euros. "To get you started."

The word "start" sounded to Blessed like a command. He gathered his plastic bag and spare shoes, the soles again concealed. Then he shook Paul's hand, kissed his own fingers, and touched them to his heart.

• • •

Ever since Blessed had left his village, his sadness had been constant. He bore it in silence, as he would a scar or a limp. But when he left the *carmen*, it boiled up inside him. He felt he had been right not to clean a room that had *zebs* scrawled on paper and a *kus* on an easel. But why, when he had done right, had he suffered this wrong?

In the Book it was written, "We will inflict upon them the

lighter punishment of this world before the supreme punishment of the world to come so that they may return to the right path." He tried to understand his mistake and Allah's will. What was the right path? From the *carmen*, every street and staircase ran downhill to Little Morocco, which looked and smelled like the world he hoped he had escaped.

He searched for work in tea shops, tattoo parlors, restaurants, and souvenir stalls that had Arabic-speaking owners. He pleaded that he could clean, he could carry heavy cartons. But no one would hire him. They saved jobs for men from their family, their tribe, their sect. Day laborers, most of them Black, slumped against walls, each holding a tool that signified his trade: a hammer for a carpenter, a wrench for a plumber, a trowel for a bricklayer, a lightbulb for an electrician.

With colored chalk, beggars sketched pictures on sidewalks. The flagstones in Plaza Nueva framed copies of church murals and museum masterpieces. To Blessed, they looked better than anything he had seen on the walls of the *carmen*. Yet nobody tipped the artists more than a couple of copper coins.

A great loneliness fell through him and never hit bottom. He had no friend except Allah and no consolation except in the Koran. "Did He not find you an orphan and give you shelter? Did He not find you in error and guide you? Did He not find you poor and enrich you?" Blessed fought not to lose faith.

He returned to the communal house where he had once lived with other refugees. Nobody remembered him, and he didn't recognize a soul. New migrants had replaced the old ones, and there was no room, not a single kind word for Blessed. Among the

Africans, there were now Yazidis from Iraq, and Uighurs fleeing the crackdown in China that had confined Muslims to concentration camps.

At Caritas, he was offered soup and bread, nothing more. The streets seethed with Black and Brown men who staked out the busiest corners and hawked wood carvings of elephants and giraffes, beaded skullcaps, lacquered boxes, tribal masks, and dyed scarves mass-produced in India. Some squatted on their heels, waiting patiently for customers. Others grabbed and shouted at pedestrians as they passed.

When Blessed, paper cup in hand, took up his old post outside the Italian *gelateria*, a burly goon demanded five euros protection money. Blessed confessed he was broke, and the goon chased him away. Every inch of pavement, every chance for profit, was subdivided and for sale. The Chinese, Blessed learned, controlled the market for fake handbags, sunglasses, and soccer shoes. Asians were reputed to be demon bosses. Still, Blessed would have worked for them if only he could have afforded to pay up front for merchandise.

As the autumn turned rainy and cold, there were fights for warm places to sleep under canopied doorways, highway overpasses, and glassed-in alcoves at ATM machines. Once you lucked into a spot, you had to pray that the police didn't roust you out. Some cops could be bribed, but Blessed hoarded the euros Paul had given him and moved on.

From time to time, he bumped into Patsy in the marketplace. She sympathized with Blessed and excoriated Paul for firing him. She gave him a little money and wished him good luck, promising they'd meet again.

Finally he found a self-storage warehouse near the train station where the manager rented empty units. For two euros, he let Blessed sleep on the concrete floor, his head pillowed on his plastic clothes bag. At dawn, before sunup, the manager banged the metal door and opened a hosepipe so that Blessed could splash freezing water over his body. He was desperate to stay clean.

Once the manager came to trust Blessed, he switched him to a unit crammed with furniture. There was a musty couch with busted springs, which was better than the floor. A scrap of carpet served as a prayer rug.

During the day, standing in line for food at Caritas, Blessed kept a tight rein on his thoughts. But at night, after he crawled into the storage unit, his mind flew out of control, his sorrow soured into rage, and devils thronged his dreams. Did anyone in his village remember him? It didn't seem possible. That was a different world, and he had forgotten why it had been so urgent to leave it. Now he was in the wrong life, where no right one was available to him.

He remembered Paul and Patsy and the artist lady. He remembered killing the snake in the garden and the videos of executions—heads thudding to the sand, throats foaming blood, the man in black threatening *toubab* nonbelievers. With some of the euros from Paul, he went to Internet cafés and paid for computer time. On Islamic websites, Believers taught how to build suicide vests. The programs were like cooking shows. Men and veiled women busied themselves in kitchens, demonstrating every step of the recipe. A bomb, he learned, was as simple to make as *pastilla*, a pigeon pie with multiple layers of pastry. The ingredients were at hand in the average home. To produce a batch of triacetone triperoxide required only hydrogen peroxide 3 percent and strong hydrochloric or sulfuric acid. Nail-polish remover was a convenient source of acetone, and a car battery could supply sulfuric acid.

"No need for a triggering device," a voiceover reassured viewers. "Once you have a white crystalline powder, you transfer it to a container. Careful to refrigerate it. You have to get it exactly right or it'll get you. TATP is the Mother of Satan—highly unstable and easily ignited by friction or a rise in temperature.

"The advantage is TATP can't be detected by sniffer dogs, and when packed with bolts and nails in a suicide vest, it has a 99 percent mortality rate at close range. It obliterates the martyr, instantly and painlessly blowing off his head." The program concluded with a sura: "'Those who are killed in the way of Allah will never let their deeds be lost.'"

Pinpricks of sweat popped out on Blessed's forehead. He noticed perspiration on the brows of other men in the Internet café. Everyone else was riveted by porn, while he questioned whether he had the courage to blow himself apart so that he could be made whole again by Allah.

CHAPTER V

A black Chevy Suburban, squat and solid as an armored personnel carrier, trundled down the road and parked almost flush with the *carmen*'s front door. A trim, close-shaved marine was at the wheel. Bill Spann slid his ponderous bulk out on the passenger side. Against the November chill, he wore a flannel shirt and quilted vest, like a deer hunter headed for the woods. He hip-bumped the door shut behind him. With its window of bulletproof Perspex, the door had the resonance of a slamming safe-deposit box.

From the SUV's back seat sprang a man as small and tight-knit as a jockey. He had leathery, sun-damaged skin but the spry manner of a middle-aged dandy in a check cashmere sport coat, a blue Lacoste shirt, khaki trousers, and tasseled loafers.

Going by Spann's description of Tahar Mahmoud as a university professor who had survived imprisonment and torture, Paul had expected someone diminished, gravely subdued. Not this grinning Algerian with a warm handshake and a perky British accent. "I travel light," he said when Paul offered help with his luggage. "I can manage on my own."

"How was the trip?" Paul asked.

"A journey full of surprises."

"We took the scenic route," Spann said.

"He means a circuitous route," Tahar said. An overnight bag in one hand, a suitcase in the other, he paused to admire the grillwork on the windows. "I imagine young girls at night whispering to their *novios* through these bars."

Spann chortled. "I picture *novios* slipping their hands between the bars and between the señoritas' legs."

"Mr. Spann is an earthy character in the Falstaff tradition," Tahar said.

Inside the *carmen*, he praised the Mudejar decor. "Perhaps you know that my hometown, Tlemcen, has some of the most magnificent examples of Moorish art and architecture in the world. The minaret of our mosque rivals the Koutoubia tower in Marrakech and the Giralda in Sevilla."

"Sounds like a beautiful city," Paul said.

"It is. But to be honest, I prefer Oxford and Cambridge."

"Let's get you settled," Spann said, "before we start beating our gums about our favorite towns."

Paul escorted them down dim corridors over faceted tiles that gleamed like the scales of a carp. Floor polish raised a faintly antiseptic smell and made for slippery footing. Paul had replaced the family portraits that used to line the walls with art donated by departing residents, much of it amateurish. Tahar's suite and separate studio were sparsely furnished with an IKEA desk, a threadbare armchair, and vacant bookshelves. Paul apologized about the crucifix on the wall above the bed and promised to remove it, but Tahar told him, "Leave it. I welcome divine inspiration whatever its source."

Spann was testing the bars on a back door that led to the courtyard. "Remember to keep this locked."

"Mr. Spann is more concerned about my safety than I am."

"That's my job. That's why Uncle Sam pays me the big bucks."

"Are you hungry?" Paul asked Tahar.

"No. But I would appreciate a cup of tea."

"Of course. How do you like it? With lemon? Mint?"

"I prefer it white. Milk, not cream. A habit I picked up during my sabbaticals in England."

"What about you, Bill?"

"I'm dying for a cigarette. How about bending the rules? The professor and I have to hunker down for a long talk, and I don't feature doing that out on the playground."

"I'll make an exception. You can smoke in the courtyard."

"It's freezing out there."

"It's not cold if you sit in the sun."

"Spain is like Algeria," Tahar said. "A cold country that just happens to have a warm sun. Nothing like the climate in the UK."

While Spann trudged out to the garden, Paul walked Tahar to the kitchen and introduced him to Patsy. The dark, diminutive couple might have hatched from the same egg. But where Tahar was nattily dressed and smiling, Patsy remained her sullen self in an apron and head scarf. "Tahar is here to finish a book," Paul explained.

"I thought he was replacing Blessed," she said.

"Hope you'll find Granada an agreeable place to work." Paul wanted to cut short any mention of Blessed in front of Tahar.

"I can write anywhere." He gazed across the table's scarred

wooden surface. "In prison, I spent hours plotting my novel. Without that diversion, I wouldn't have survived."

Patsy served him cookies on a saucer with his tea. "Peek Freans," Tahar exclaimed. "I haven't had one since my last stay in England."

"When was that?" Paul asked.

"Back when the UK still welcomed academic exchanges with Algeria. That ended in the '90s, when terrorists scared the government into declaring an emergency and canceling elections."

Tahar blew to cool his tea. When he lifted a membrane of milk from its surface, his fingers had a slight tremor, and the nails on both hands were missing. "Authorities feared that if the Islamists took power, they'd turn the country into a caliphate under sharia law. One man, one vote, one time. No more elections, no more freedom of dissent.

"Two hundred thousand people died in a war that the world was hardly aware of. It ended in exhaustion with an armistice and an amnesty for terrorists. Just as things were improving, Al-Qaeda crashed those planes into the World Trade Center, and that killed any chance of my traveling to England ever again."

Tahar pinched at the creases of his trousers, smoothing imaginary wrinkles.

Paul said, "Sorry," aware of how absurdly inadequate this sounded. Then Spann shouted from the courtyard, and Tahar followed Paul out to where the fat man sat flicking cigarette ashes in the general direction of the fountain. The koi mistook the ashes for food and rose to gulp them. Spann swiped one of Tahar's Peek Freans and popped it into his mouth. "Let's get down to business."

• • •

Simone referred to her daily walks with Paul as "adventures." They strayed far from the grueling boulevards of modern Granada into obscure bends and elbows of the city. No matter how much they meandered, Paul had a sense that they were going someplace, getting closer to something.

"Where's Blessed?" Simone asked.

"I sent him away."

"Thanks."

This caused him a twinge of guilt, but he was happy to have her believe he had done it for her. "An Algerian writer just checked in. He's applied for asylum in the States. The US Embassy decided to interview him here. I thought it'd hurt Blessed to have another African receive royal treatment while he's scuffling to get by. So I put him on leave."

"You're such a softy."

"So my father always said."

"Tell me about him. You described him as a story for a rainy day. But don't they claim sunlight's the best disinfectant?"

"What gives you the idea memories of my father need to be disinfected?"

"Just guessing."

"I'd rather hear about your family."

"No, you wouldn't. They were white-bread Upper East Siders." In a Fair Isle cardigan, her eyes masked by mirror-lens Ray-Bans, Simone resembled a trophy wife swanning past shops on Madison Avenue. She didn't appear to take particular notice of anything. She never carried a sketch pad or camera. "My parents were like characters—no, caricatures—from a John Cheever story," she said. "My mother by all accounts, including her own, was a gifted dancer, a gourmet cook, a terrific organizer of parties. These days, she'd probably earn a fortune as an event planner or an influencer."

"What was she like as a mother?"

"She didn't have much interest in kids until they were old enough to mix a perfect martini."

Paul laughed. "At what age did you become her bartender?"

"I drew the line at that. But when I was a teenager and our feet were the same size, she convinced me to wear her new shoes. She didn't want to get blisters. So she had me break them in for her. I felt very grown-up in Italian designer high heels."

They skirted a wall of stones dating from different eras, fitted together like patches on a quilt, and advanced under a horseshoe arch into Plaza Larga. Workers were clamorously dismantling the metal frames of a vegetable market. Other men, even noisier, hawked the last baskets of oranges and olives.

"I bet your father doted on you," Paul said.

"He did when he was home. He was away a lot. Up in the air."

"Head in the clouds?"

"Literally in the clouds. He was an airline pilot. I didn't see much of him."

"Poor baby."

"Aren't you sweet."

"You mean soft."

"No, just the right degree of empathy."

Their exchanges had a rhythm that reminded Paul of child

hood days when Virtudes set him on his feet and urged him, "*Baila, baila.*" Dance, dance.

They reached Sacramonte, where the hillsides were honeycombed with caves and plastered with ads for flamenco shows. Two men on motor scooters zipped past, dressed in ruffled shirts and tight trousers, guitars slung across their backs.

"There were advantages to having an airline pilot in the family," Simone said. "I got free tickets anywhere in the world. When I was fifteen, my mother booked me on Air France to Paris with a message for my father. He was there with his mistress. The message was 'Fly home or I'll divorce you.' He put me on the next flight back to New York with his reply, 'My lawyer will contact yours.'"

"I remember times like that, tiptoeing on a high wire between my mother and father. My parents' divorce was like the Spanish Civil War, a never-ending anthology of atrocities." He meant this to be funny, but it sounded so lachrymose that he added, "Unfortunately, the national Pact of Forgetting never extended to family matters."

"You should write a book about your childhood in Granada," Simone suggested.

"My father's example killed that urge. He always claimed to be working on a book. I think his writing was another way to get laid."

Simone's response seemed a strenuous failure to react.

"Hey, here I am whining about my family," Paul said, "when I wanted to hear about yours."

A November night swooped down on them, powered by a cold wind from the Sierra Nevada. Dead leaves skittered around their feet. Back in the Albaicín, there was the smell of cedar logs in fireplaces and kebabs hissing on braziers. To escape the wind, they stopped for a glass of Tuareg tea thick with mint leaves and sugar.

Not long ago, the bars in this neighborhood had reeked of cigarette smoke and had blared televised soccer matches. Now there was moody light and Gnaoua music on tape. Simone and Paul crouched cross-legged on hassocks at a hammered brass table.

"I've read," Simone said, "that Granada used to be the gateway that funneled Islamic sensuality into sad-sack Catholic Spain."

"That's the cliché. The steamy sway of the harem. Hash hallucinations. Jasmine-scented sex. Edward Said debunked all that in *Orientalism*."

"Never read it. Does the book describe how centuries of Arabic art and architecture ended up in this swamp of kitsch?"

"We live in a fallen world," Paul said in mock seriousness. "Still, the authentic Eastern experience exists. Like to travel with me to Samarkanda?"

"That's the most romantic offer I've had in months. Where do I sign up?"

"What you do is follow me."

With a hand from Paul, she uncoiled from the hassock, and once they were outside, she slipped her arm through his.

"Samarkanda's a restaurant," Paul said. "Short on ambience, but the food's terrific."

He had eaten there off and on for years, and the owner greeted him warmly and wasn't insulted when Paul pointed out that instead of photos of the Cedars of Lebanon, he should have displayed shots of Tamburlaine's tomb in Uzbekistan. He gave them a corner table covered with a plain white cloth and paper napkins. "Here you can be private," he said.

But the owner didn't leave them alone. He stuck around and recounted tales Paul had heard before. How he had fled the Middle East when Beirut was suffering one of its periodic spasms of ethnic violence. How he didn't resent the newly arrived Iraqi and Syrian restaurateurs. "We are all brothers," he insisted, "not competitors. Anyway, I am famous and have many, many customers. It's early now. You'll see them later."

As proof of his celebrity, he fetched a framed article from the *New York Times* travel section. A small service box recommended his restaurant as a dependable spot for a reasonably priced meal.

Paul reminded him that they were hungry, and the owner fetched dishes of dolmas and hummus and *moutabal* and a bottle of red Lebanese wine. Then at last he retreated to the kitchen.

"Does he cook," Simone asked, "as well as wait tables and tell his life story?"

"He's lonely and craves company."

"He'll be fine once the dinner crowd shows up." She gestured at the empty room. "Let's take advantage of the privacy and tell each other our secret life stories."

"You go first."

She nibbled hummus off a wedge of pita bread. "I have an ex-husband."

"That strikes me as a banal bit of information, not a deep, dark secret."

"What about you? Is there a wife, current or former, somewhere out of sight?"

"Nope." He poured the wine, which appeared to be purple, unlike the usual blood-red Spanish vintages. "Where's your ex?"

"In Florida. He's a biologist."

"I can't picture you with a scientist, living near a golf course in a gated community."

"We lived in the Keys, surrounded by mangroves. It was pretty primitive, but at least we had AC."

"So you holed up in your air-conditioned studio and painted whatever naked exhibitionists happened to pop up on your computer screen?"

"No, this was before I found my voice, my subject. Back then, I did sunsets and seascapes. Meanwhile, my husband collected specimens. The problem was he brought them home. Our yard was like Jurassic Park. We had sea turtles and iguanas and even a monitor lizard. Some fool kept it as a pet until it got big enough to bite his hand off."

"Sounds like my father."

"I thought he was a university professor."

This gave him pause. He didn't remember telling her that. Maybe she had inferred as much from something Paul had said. "Yeah, that's what he did when he wasn't chasing women or flying off to the Caribbean. He came home from one of his trips with a baby ocelot and penned it in the backyard."

"Where was this?"

"In Florida, near the campus."

"Didn't the neighbors complain?"

"No, it was so small and cuddly at first, you could hold it in your cupped hands. It had beautiful spots and black stripes on its tail. But when it got bigger—"

"How big?"

Paul estimated the ocelot's length with one arm. "About three feet from nose to tail. It weighed over thirty pounds. It ate raw meat, ripped it apart with its teeth. Dad chained its collar to an overhead clothesline so it could run back and forth in the yard and get exercise but couldn't attack anybody."

"Were you scared of it?"

"Dad warned me that I'd better be. As soon as the ocelot got big enough to hunt, it began stalking me. The worst part was its smell. Dad said he'd rather get bitten by an ocelot than shit on by one."

"Some choice. Why would anyone keep an animal like that?"

"Why did your husband keep a monitor lizard?"

"Maybe, like your father, he thought of himself as a tamer of wild beasts."

Paul doubted his father had ever considered taming the ocelot—any more than he had ever bothered taming his own appetites. More likely, he derived perverse pleasure from teaching his son a lesson anything as beautiful and vicious as an ocelot was bound to foul whatever it didn't devour.

When their chicken shashlik and basmati rice arrived, Paul suggested a second bottle of wine. Simone said, "Let's wait and have a glass of white with dessert. What became of the ocelot?"

"The next time I visited Florida, the cat was gone."

"No explanation?"

"My father was a never-explain, never-complain kind of guy. When he got tired of something, he got rid of it."

This sounded harsher than he had intended and suffused Simone's cheeks with color. "How about your ex?" he asked. "Are you in touch with him?"

"He's out of the picture. Some men you never forget. Other men fall out of your head as soon as the heavy breathing stops."

Paul wondered which category he fit in. Most men, he supposed, liked to believe no woman could ever forget them. But in his experience, there were instances when amnesia was a blessing on both sides.

"Ever see the green flash in Florida?" Simone asked, recalling something as transient as her husband.

"Not in Florida. But down in the islands, I saw it. Not that Dad believed me. He argued that the green rays have to be vertical. Not horizontal."

"Funny," she said, "I had the same experience. Why are men so controlling? So dead set on defining things for you?"

"Don't look at me. I'm laid back."

"That's what they all say at the start."

The dinner crowd never materialized; Samarkanda's owner blamed the weather. It had started raining, and as Simone and Paul stepped outside, it poured down in straight lines, stinging their faces like sleet. She thrust her arm through his and clung tight as they skidded across Plaza Nueva, where the wet stones were as slippery as soap. The rain beat on the abandoned café tables and on the roof of the taxi they caught. During the zigzag climb to the *carmen*, Simone was thrown against Paul at every curve, and he felt her shivering under her soaked Fair Isle sweater.

Patsy hadn't bothered to leave a light on. Moving by touch, Paul untumbled the front door lock, and he and Simone ducked into the hallway, where the instant he switched on a lamp, the ex-voto body parts on the walls took shape like an anatomy lesson. Tahar was asleep in his room. The house was as silent as a museum after hours.

Paul pried off his sopping shoes, and Simone did the same. Their wet socks left perfect footprints on the tiles. "Cold," she whispered through chattering teeth.

"I'll bring you a plug-in heater."

"Don't bother." At the door to her suite, she said, "Like to come in and keep me warm?"

There was no more talk, no glib banter. After a kiss, she vanished into the bathroom, and he undressed and slid under the covers. Now his teeth were chattering too. He wouldn't call it performance anxiety exactly, but the collage of cocks in the room and two new canvases of female nudes left him uneasy. Why Simone chose to paint what she did might be as simple as easy access to Internet models, plus a determination to tip centuries of masculine sexual assumptions upside down. But Paul thought that her appetites might be as powerful as his desire was at the moment.

Simone emerged from the bathroom and shed a silk robe. She clicked off the lights and crawled in beside him. There was a powerful personal scent that he dredged in like a drug. Whatever he touched—her flanks, her breasts, her belly—was as cool as marble and as smooth. But when he moved his hand between her legs, her flesh was warm and giving.

She touched him, and he said, "If you'll keep your hands to yourself and lie very still, this will only take about thirty seconds."

Laughter shook her upper body, but her hand stayed where it was. "A joke'll help you once, maybe twice, but in the end, you better come through."

He knelt between her legs, and she raised her knees. For a moment, he hesitated, and she said, "I want to feel you inside me. Don't wait for me. I like to get right up to the edge and linger there for a while."

In contrast to what her art had led him to expect, sex with Simone was in no way unconventional except for her eagerness to return to talking. She switched on the lights and tossed back the covers. "I knew I was right to want to paint you. You have a beautiful cock."

"Is that what you call it?" They were back to teasing and taunting.

"What do you call it?"

"I'm not big on nicknames."

"What's your position on pussy?"

"I'm in favor."

"I'm asking a serious question."

"Do you mean the word? Or the thing itself?"

"The word."

He glanced down at Simone, who was Brazilian-waxed. "It's not applicable in your case."

"That's not the question. When is the word permissible in polite conversation? Everybody's mixed up these days, even TV commentators. When they talk about that Russian girl band, they say 'Pussy Riot.' But when Trump bragged about where he grabs women, they bleeped it out."

"A true conundrum." He tucked his hand back between her thighs. "I think it's time you quit lingering at the edge."

CHAPTER VI

Tahar lay open-eyed on a firm, clean mattress. Outside, frigid air sighed against the windows while he was warmed by a feather duvet. Unlike his prison cot, which had been rank with sweat, urine, and an almost animal odor of fear, his bed at the residency smelled of freshly starched sheets. Yet now, just as then, he fought against a trapped, smothering panic and against pain that never completely disappeared. At times it retreated deep into his bones, but it never stayed buried. It burst out of him, usually when he let down his guard just before he slept.

He had attempted to describe this pain to Bill Spann, only to have the odious US Embassy official insist on facts, not feelings. This was unlike their encounters before he had come to Spain. Back then, Spann had exuded sympathy and interest in everything to do with Tahar's plight. But today in the courtyard, he had concentrated on terrorism with a capital T, not the personal terror Tahar had suffered. He demanded actionable intelligence about the torturers, nothing about the rampant gradations of pain they had inflicted, nothing about the distinctions between waterboarding and being hoisted from a rafter by his elbows, between being force-fed or forced to submit to an enema.

"Start at the beginning," Spann had badgered him. "Gimme details."

"God is in the details." Tahar studied the goldfish in the fountain as they gobbled Spann's cigarette ashes. He tasted ashes, felt them grate in his eyes.

"I thought the devil was in the details," Spann said. "Tell me about the torturers' faces. Distinctive features. Scars."

"Maybe if you showed me photographs, I'd recognize them."

"Jihadis don't do selfies. Tell me about their race. Were they Black, white, Brown?"

"All of the above. The cast of characters changed day to day. They switched roles."

"You make it sound like a stage play, a spectacle."

"That's how it felt. Like they had rehearsed everything in advance."

"Some of these groups," Spann agreed, "see themselves as choreographers. In Chile, they call the torture chamber 'the blue-lit stage.' In the Philippines, it's 'the production room.' In Vietnam, it was 'the cinema room.'"

"What do Americans call the torture room?"

"We don't torture."

"Okay, have it your way. What's the word for the enhanced interrogation room?"

"We're wandering off the subject. Were your torturers North Africans?"

"How could I possibly tell?"

"By their accents. Did they speak Berber or a local dialect?"

"Among themselves, they spoke a bit of everything. But they interrogated me in Arabic."

"Street Arabic? Or classical?"

"Street Arabic. There was slang I didn't understand. They shouted at me and slapped me and slammed me against the wall. I couldn't keep their voices straight."

"Did any of them speak French?"

"A few."

"Did they sound like native French speakers?"

"I'd just be guessing."

"Hey, you're a professor of philology. Language is your field. Go ahead and guess."

"They yelled too fast and loud, like you're doing now."

"I'm not yelling." Spann softened his voice. "Just trying to get your attention."

"These days, I have trouble concentrating. My ears ache and my head hurts and I don't sleep at night."

"Join the club. You think I sleep, knowing what's out there? Knowing what we're up against? Knowing I don't know the half of it?"

"Nobody sleeps in heaven," Tahar replied. "Nobody, nobody, nobody is sleeping."

"You can fucking say that again."

Spann lit a fresh cigarette off the one in his mouth and French-inhaled. Tahar remembered students doing that at Oxford, imitating Jean-Paul Belmondo in *Breathless*. He doubted Spann was familiar with French films or that he recognized the poem Tahar continued to recite:

"Let there be a landscape of open eyes
And bitter wounds on fire.
No one is sleeping in the world.
No one, no one."

"Are you doing this to piss me off?" Spann demanded.

"You don't like Lorca?"

"What I'd like is a few straight answers. Tell me again about your kidnapping."

"First, you have to understand the context, the predicament of university professors in Algeria."

Spann expelled a tobacco-fouled breath. "You must have bored your students shitless."

"These things can't be hurried. To understand the present, you need to know the past. You can't judge my petition for asylum unless you realize where I was raised. I'm from a city that used to be one of the most tolerant in the world. We granted sanctuary to Jews and Christians during the Inquisition."

"All due respect, Professor, we're going round and round. I want to hear what happened to you, not to your hometown."

"The two can't be separated. What terrorism did to me, it also did to Tlemcen. It was like a strangler fig, choking off our life. The Triangle of Death blocked us from Algiers and Oran. The roads all had checkpoints and you couldn't guess whether they were guarded by genuine soldiers or Islamists wearing stolen uniforms. Tlemcen was deserted and the mosque locked its doors after the night prayer and we hid in our houses. Some students I taught during the day joined the jihadis after dark."

"All very interesting, very suggestive." Spann's cigarette butt hissed as it hit the fishpond. "But the folks who pay me insist on concrete information."

"What's more concrete than the fatwa against me? For that alone, I deserve asylum."

"Asylum isn't all you're asking for," Spann responded. "You're angling for a job at an American university. For your book to be published in the US. For medical care. In case it hasn't occurred to you, the National Security Agency isn't a charitable organization. It's strictly give and get."

Tahar dredged in the smell of the garden's dead flowers and vines, its damp irrigation ditches. He debated whether to drop his trousers and demonstrate what the Islamists had done to him.

"To the best of your recollection," Spann started over, "what led to your kidnapping?"

"The Groupe Islamique Armé issued a decree that female students should cover their hair and wear the hijab. I was supposed to enforce the rule in my classes. I refused because I knew the government would arrest me if I obeyed the GIA. There was no safe path."

"So you didn't go along with the GIA, and they grabbed you."

"The GIA or another group. It could have been ISIS or AQIM. I was a perfect target. An English-speaking intellectual. A relic of French colonialism. Jean-Paul Sartre described men like me as being branded 'with a red-hot iron, with principles of western culture.'"

"Leave Sartre out of this. Stick to your own experience."

"Okay, I was drinking tea at a café on Place Mohamed Khemisti, in front of the Grand Mosque. A van bumped up over the curb."

"What make? What model?"

"I can't say. It was all so quick. Someone knocked me unconscious, and I revived on the floor of the van with a hood over my head. I smelled ripe vegetables and figured we were in the souk. Then the smell changed to broken bricks, and I knew we were in Kabul."

"Kabul! What the fuck?" Spann's freshly lit cigarette fell onto his lap, and he slapped it away before it burned a hole in his pants.

"Kabul is what we called an area of Tlemcen that had been bombed out and never rebuilt," Tahar explained.

"How long were you in the van?"

"I'd estimate an hour. I heard the tires on cobblestones, then on asphalt and guessed we were still in the city. When there was the sound of gravel, I figured we were in the country. They stopped and dragged me inside what smelled like a barn."

"Do you mean it smelled like manure or like chemical fertilizer?"

"What difference does it make?"

"Certain terrorists improvise bombs out of chemical fertilizer. It could help specify the group."

"To me, it smelled like animal waste," Tahar said.

"Did you notice any pipes? Metal containers? Wires? Any ingredients for IEDs?"

"I had the hood on. They didn't remove it until I was in a cell."

"Were there bars? A cage?"

"No, the walls were solid cinder block, the door a sheet of steel. There were no windows. The only light was on the ceiling, far too high for me to reach. They left it on at night so I couldn't sleep."

"Did you have a watch?"

"No. They stole it."

"How could you tell if it was night or day?"

"I couldn't. They kept me disoriented, waking me up at odd hours. Sometimes torturing me. Sometimes not. There was no pattern. I never knew what to expect."

"Describe the cell."

"Walls. A cement floor. A corrugated iron roof."

"Did they chain you to the cot?"

"Only when I was being waterboarded. The rest of the time I was free to move around. At first, I tried to exercise and stay alert. I read what was written on the walls."

"Written with what? By who?"

"Other prisoners. They scratched words with their fingernails. Some wrote in blood after their nails were ripped out."

"Was it Arabic?"

"Yes, mostly. A bit of French."

"Anything in English?"

"Not that I remember."

"Wouldn't something in English stick in your mind?"

"There were periods when I think I lost my mind."

"Do you remember anything that was written on the walls?"

"Verses from the Koran. '*La ilaha Illallah.* There is no God but Allah.' That sort of thing."

"Did you write anything?"

"I'm an agnostic."

"I'm not talking about prayers. Did you scratch your name in your cell? Anything that could distinguish the place?"

Tahar shook his head.

Spann stamped his feet, perhaps in inpatience, perhaps because of the cold. "You were locked up almost a year. Didn't anything stand out?"

"The drawings stood out."

"Drawings of what?"

"Stick figures of men and women fucking. One picture had a quote from the Koran: 'Women are your fields; go then into your fields as you please.'"

"I'm a farm boy. I know a thing or two about plowing. And I have a sixth sense when people are shoveling horseshit."

"I answered everything honestly." Tahar pushed up off the cold lip of the fountain. "Maybe you need to ask better questions."

"Look, Professor, I'm not here to play games. You contacted us. You volunteered. Next time, you better step up to the plate and belt the ball out of the park."

• • •

No one sleeps. No one in the world. Lorca's lyric was an earworm as Tahar stared at the dark overhead beams of his bedroom, bold against the whitewashed ceiling. He left the light on; prison had habituated him to this. He dropped off for a few moments and woke with a start. Pain and panic poured through him. His hair ached right down to its roots. He feared he was back in the cell with guards waiting for him to open his eyes so they could slap them shut again.

Every day of captivity had commenced with cruelty. If Tahar was hungry, the guards taunted him with food but wouldn't let him eat. If he insisted he had no appetite, they force-fed him until he vomited. If he complained of thirst, they flung a chiffon over his face and emptied a bucket of water into his nose and mouth until he nearly drowned. To prevent water intoxication and seizures, they injected a saline solution and rehydrated him rectally.

His body no longer belonged to him. They owned him, inside and out. If he woke with an erection, they attached his testicles to what they called a telephone and turned on the electrical current. It scorched his groin and singed his pubic hair. It felt . . . No, he couldn't describe how it felt. Pain at that level resisted language, destroyed it altogether.

• • •

Next morning at the *carmen*, Tahar reached down and touched his privates, testing whether they were still there. On the wall above his head, a tiny, almost transparent lizard rocked up and down, as if doing push-ups. He heaved back the duvet and stepped into the bathroom. Lathering his cheeks, he tugged a razor against the grain of his whiskers. To set himself apart from Islamists, he never grew a beard. He also kept his hair cropped short. This was a secret vanity. Whenever it grew long, as it had during his captivity, the guards mocked Tahar as a man of Black ancestry.

He never deluded himself that he could pass for British. Still, it meant a great deal to him to speak and dress the part. On his sabbaticals, he had developed discerning tastes. He could distinguish cashmere from merino wool and authentic John Lobb shoes from cheap imitations.

In other respects, Tahar had humble needs and abstemious appetites. Prison food—or was it torture?—had left him with little hunger. A sip of wine acted on him like an insult to the brain. Two sips were as bad as having his head rammed against the cell wall. As for sex, he assumed the telephone had killed all desire.

Walking to the kitchen, Tahar felt that the *carmen*, despite its Moorish decor, resembled a Catholic church—the scent of candle wax and wine, a hush he violated as his tasseled loafers clacked against ceramic tiles. He paused in the library and spotted a copy of *The Secret Agent* by Joseph Conrad. The book jacket described it as a portrait of terror in England in the early twentieth century, when law enforcement agents often seemed interchangeable with the revolutionaries they pursued. Hoping for help with his own fiction, he took the paperback.

At the table, Paul sat opposite an attractive woman. To Tahar, they looked like they had recently rolled out of bed. Together? Separately? Paul was dressed. The woman wore a brightly striped caftan as a robe.

"I borrowed a book from the library," Tahar said.

Paul introduced Simone Pierce to Professor Mahmoud. "Visual artist, meet writer."

"Please, call me Tahar!" He watched Simone fill a cup with coffee to the brim. To keep it from spilling, she lowered her head and pursed her lips as if in a kiss. Her eyes had minute flecks of green sea ice.

"Is your writing set in Granada?" Simone asked.

"No, in Algeria. I'm really just starting. For an artist, Granada must be a great inspiration."

"Inspiration is exaggerated," she replied with a smile that melted the ice from her eyes. "Philip Roth claimed that novels aren't made of inspiration. They're made out of words. I guess for an artist, the equivalent is images."

"Images are also important to writers. Chateaubriand said, '*J'allais chercher des images, tout voilà*.'" Although Tahar feared sounding like a pedant, he felt surer of himself when quoting a source.

"I'm looking for models. Could I interest you in posing?"

"Jesus, Simone, the man just got here," Paul said. "He hasn't even eaten breakfast."

He called out to Patsy, who stepped from the supply closet, stern as a schoolmarm, her mouth cinched as if by a drawstring. Grudgingly she relit the stove and rinsed out the coffee pot.

"Did the others eat earlier?" Tahar asked.

"There are no others," Paul said. "We're sailing with a skeleton crew. Just you, Simone, and me."

"What a sly one you are," Simone teased Tahar. "You haven't answered my question about posing and haven't said a word about your novel."

"I'm afraid I'm not really model material. I'm much too homely. As for my novel, it's a retelling of André Gide's *The Immoralist* from the point of view of an Arab boy who's sexually exploited and turns into a terrorist."

"Spann's under the impression that you're rewriting Camus's *The Plague*," Paul said.

"That's precisely why I'm reluctant to discuss a work in progress." Tahar sounded abjectly apologetic. "The Camus elements have somehow faded, and to my surprise, Gide and the theme of sex and terrorism have taken over."

Patsy brought him breakfast on a tray, and Tahar said he'd eat at his desk while working. But once in his studio, he stood at the barred window, staring out at the dying garden. In prison, he had regretted not having a window. Now he realized that a blank wall could be a blessing and an alibi for writer's block.

His hope had been that a stay at an arts residency would allow him to learn from published authors. He had envisioned long talks about technique, discussions of narrative devices. He was a complete novice at fiction—unless you counted his correspondence with the US Embassy in Madrid. Now he didn't know how to get started.

Tahar booted up his computer and searched several Internet sites for aspiring novelists. When he typed in key words—"terrorism," "Islamic radicals," "suicide bombers"—an entry for Ayad el-Baghdadi appeared on the screen. He was identified as an Arab Spring activist who had defined the seven steps to radicalization:

1. Otherization: I am of one group, they are from another.
2. Collectivization: They are all the same.
3. Oppression narrative: They are oppressing us.
4. Collective guilt: They are all complicit in oppressing us.
5. Supremacism narrative: We are better than them.
6. Self-defense: We have to retaliate against their aggression.
7. The idea of violence: Violence is the only way.

CHAPTER VII

Autumn ended with a series of thunderstorms—*tormentas*, the locals called them—and rain fell in silver chains strung with drops the size of pearls. Parched ground drank up the first torrents, then, when it could absorb no more, water flooded downhill, spreading a layer of orange mud into the Darro River. Throughout the city, sewers brimmed and overflowed; rainwater spilled from rooftops and ran in braids over the cobblestones.

Patsy cowered in the kitchen, whispering prayers for protection against lightning. Paul had witnessed these spasms of superstition in the past and persuaded her to translate her Creole imprecations: "Saint Barbara, generous virgin, give me the life you lived, free from the death you died."

"Was Saint Barbara killed by lightning?" Paul asked.

"No, her father murdered her."

"I'm familiar with such fathers," he said. But Patsy was not amused.

The foul weather didn't dent Simone's coltish high spirits. She claimed that her work went well, rain or shine. For an artist whose painting was so deeply transgressive, she had the cheerfulness of a Hallmark card designer. Paul assumed that she stayed in touch by email or video call with her agent, various galleries, and friends in the States. But she never referred to her online activities beyond observing again that she had no shortage of models.

This didn't, however, stop her from nagging Paul to pose for her. And he continued to refuse. Why should he join the anonymous figures stick-pinned to her walls? At the core of his affability, there was a stubborn streak that resisted following the crowd. He always held something of himself back, just as he suspected Simone did.

She stayed on at the *carmen* week after week and paid in cash at the end of each month. She never mentioned how long she planned to remain there, and he didn't ask. The question that hovered over the whole affair was how long it would last. Similar questions, and the tensions they provoked, loomed over other aspects of his life. The survival of his arts residence, the deterioration of the *carmen* itself all added to an uncertainty that had become constant. Although he never expressed this in words, he had the sense that his whole way of life could be lost.

Paul's flings with previous residents—few and far between as he preferred to believe they had been—had lasted a couple of weeks, a month at most. Several women had declared that they loved him and swore to return or to rendezvous with him the next time he was in New York. This had never happened. He hadn't let it happen.

To those who accused him of being commitment-phobic, he replied that his commitment was to the querencia he had inherited, to an ongoing romance with the Albaicín. As in any marriage, there had been low moments; there had been breakups and emotional reconciliations. But he had never considered leaving Granada, and insofar as he had future plans, he couldn't conceive of them apart from it.

Now Simone was another thing he was anxious not to lose. He didn't like to think of his life without her. She and Paul never mentioned this. Much as they spoke about other matters, some subjects remained out of bounds. He presumed she had had plenty of affairs, perhaps a lover still in the States, but he never probed. Nor did he attempt to winkle out of her what she had heard about him before she had come to Spain.

In bed, their vocabulary was pared back to the minimum, and they devised no secret code to camouflage their desires. Simone was explicit about what she wanted and what she didn't. She laid down few limits, but she had her preferences. She made it clear that she was more interested in receiving oral sex than giving it, and anal was entirely off the agenda. She showed him that she liked to play rough. She bit his lips and yanked his hair. She arched her spine like a bow so that he felt cords of muscle quiver inside her. She pulled him in so deep that he struck bone.

He didn't respond in kind. He had witnessed his father assault too many women to find sadism, even the soft-core variety, exciting. He watched Simone role-play and wondered whether performance art was part of her repertoire. More tantalizing, was she faking the obsessiveness of her art? In the end, did it matter as long as she stayed?

• • •

At Thanksgiving, Simone insisted on cooking dinner and sent Patsy to buy a turkey at the open market. She brought one home complete with giblets and gizzards and guts. Maybe she expected Simone to step aside and let her clean out the carcass. Instead, showing no signs of squeamishness, Simone did that and stuffed it with sausage dressing while Patsy stood glaring at her.

Or was she glaring at Tahar? From the first, she hadn't liked him. She viewed him as the man who had cruelly supplanted Blessed. As she complained to Paul, she even despised Tahar's table manners, the way he wielded his utensils *à l'anglaise.* With a knife in one hand, he mashed food onto the back of his fork and daintily lifted it to his lips.

That night in bed, Simone whispered, "Patsy hates me. She knows about us."

"I don't think so."

"She washes the sheets. Of course she knows."

"I'll tell her you're sleeping with Tahar."

"There's an idea," she said. "He's not bad-looking. Small but perfectly formed. He could improve my French."

"Why not let me teach you Spanish?"

As they lay naked in the cooling room, she lifted a shapely leg and gestured for Paul to do the same. "Mine's as long as yours. We could be brother and sister. Fraternal twins separated at birth. We both have beautiful legs."

"Mine are hairy and pale," he pointed out. "Yours are smooth and tan."

"Fake tan," she confessed and let her leg collapse over his hips. "I think I'm getting sweet on you. A schoolgirl crush."

"I'll invite you to the prom."

"You remind me of one of my grad school professors." For the first time, she violated their unspoken pact against discussing previous relationships.

"Did you fall madly in love with him?"

"Well, I fell into bed with him."

"Did he mentor you? Did he influence your art?"

"Yeah, he did all that. Then he ruined everything by becoming too possessive. In bed, he never closed his eyes. I felt like a watched pot."

Paul shut his eyes. "I can take a hint."

"No, don't. I like your eyes. I like a lot of things about you. Why won't you let me paint you?"

"You'll lose respect for me, and I'll lose my soul."

"This is as silly as your refusing to take me to the Alhambra."

• • •

Once a week, Spann arrived without the armored SUV and marine escort but always with a cigarette in his mouth and his eyes hooded against smoke.

"When did intelligence agents start to resemble the Michelin Man?" Simone asked Paul. "What happened to the James Bond look?"

"Shame on you for fat-shaming a man who probably has a glandular problem."

"Spann's problem is his personality. Tahar tells me his diplomatic skills are rotten. Being interviewed by him is worse than the third degree."

It puzzled Paul that Tahar had confided in Simone. When had they had a chance to be alone together? But it didn't disappoint him that the debriefing wasn't running smoothly. The longer it lasted, the more money Spann owed him.

• • •

After one session with Tahar, Spann vented his frustration to Paul while Patsy skulked in a corner of the kitchen listening. "All he gives me is academic gobbledygook."

"Maybe you're not asking the right questions."

"That's a line straight out of his mouth. Plus I'm damn tired of forking over ten thousand bucks a month to interrogate him on the tundra. At least let us talk indoors."

Paul relented, and Spann met Tahar in his room with the windows open to let out the cigarette smoke.

• • •

Then the weather changed, and winter sun scattered the clouds and drained the sky of color. A skimmed-milk haze hung over the city. The bougainvillea turned bone brown, the oleanders black. Wisteria and Virginia creeper vines swung in the wind like drying fishnets. The scent of fresh-cut spruce trees heralded the approach of Christmas, drenching Paul in memories of Virtudes and of the Advent calendars she had peeled open each day to reveal scenes of Joseph and Mary and baby Jesus in a Bethlehem that resembled Sacramonte, with a Gypsy cave sheltering the Holy Family.

The season also brought back less pleasant memories of school breaks he had spent in Florida with his father. Because Christmas meant nothing to Peter Stewart, Paul didn't bother with decorations or gifts—unlike Simone, who eagerly celebrated the holidays. From Plaza Larga, she lugged home a poinsettia and a potted cedar the size of a bonsai tree. She festooned the cedar with tinsel and placed it at one end of the kitchen table and the poinsettia at the other.

She volunteered to cook another turkey on Christmas Eve, but Patsy wouldn't hear of it. A *bardamerda*, Patsy muttered. Get that shit out of here. Savagely clashing pots and pans, she prepared *consoada*, a Portuguese specialty of cod with everything—boiled eggs, boiled kale, boiled potatoes, boiled onions, and chopped raw garlic all drizzled with olive oil. For dessert, she fixed *fil hoses,* deep-fried flour dough and eggs with sugar and cinnamon sprinkled on top. Rather than listen to carols while she worked, she played tapes of Cesária Évora singing *mornas*, sad laments of loss and regret.

"Nothing like a little mood music," Simone said, "to make you slit your wrists."

Tahar said, "She's had a hard life."

"How do you know?"

"We talked today. I'm not sure I got everything, but I gather she lost a child. It may have been murdered. Or maybe she had an abortion. She told me, I think, that when a child dies before it's born, the mother must carry its soul in her mouth."

"Jesus," Simone exclaimed. "A crazy alt-right antiabortionist is cooking us Christmas dinner."

When Patsy announced that the meal was ready, Simone invited her to join them at the table. Patsy brusquely refused. Still, Simone handed her a gift as she left.

Simone had bought a gift for Tahar too, a silk scarf in a paisley pattern. Then she presented Paul with a garment bag from a shop on Calle Reyes Católicos. In it was a buttery-soft leather jacket that fit him as tight as a glove. "You look like a metrosexual hipster," she said.

"I feel like a heel for not remembering a gift for you."

"It's not too late. I know what I want. Take me to midnight mass."

He thought she was joking, but Simone insisted. "I bet as a boy, you went every year."

"Yeah. Back then, religion was a defense against my father. Now that he's dead, what's the point?"

"Do it for me," she said.

This touched him, as did Tahar's plea to accompany them to church. For a few minutes, they debated whether to break Spann's edict against Tahar leaving the *carmen*. In the end, they decided against it.

Arm in arm, Simone and he strolled through the empty, wind-whistling streets to San Miguel Bajo. The starless night was as black as coal slurry. But snow was falling up in the Sierra Nevada, Paul would have bet his life on that.

The church, heated by the packed bodies of parishioners, swarmed with reminders of his childhood. The statue of Saint Michael, sword in hand, stomping on the head of a lizard-like Satan. The guttering candles, the incense, and the Gregorian chant gave him pleasure very close to pain. Churchgoing had always prompted in Paul as much guilt as exaltation.

Tonight, Black and Brown people were scattered amid the congregation. They called Blessed to his mind. Paul hoped that Blessed would find peace and grace, as the priest put it. Ill-clothed, ill-fed, simply ill, they looked to Paul as if they had stepped in here to escape the street. During the collection, they averted their eyes, as if it hurt them to see so much money and not be able to touch it.

Simone jostled his elbow and urged him to translate the sermon. Whispering into the tender shell of her ear, he tried to give her the gist of what the priest said.

A monk, long isolated in a cell, had a vision that there existed somewhere on earth a door that led directly to paradise. Spiritually arid after many years of praying and fasting, the monk abandoned his cell and set forth in search of this heavenly door. Traveling from country to country, continent to continent, he finally found it and with great eagerness opened it—only to discover himself back in his cell.

"The lesson is clear," the priest concluded. "The door of salvation, the entrance to paradise, was right in front of him all along, just as it is for you. And so the monk settled back into his holy life as a hermit."

"He's talking about you in your tower," Simone murmured.

• • •

When they resumed their daily walks after the first of the year, the sky was so bright that they blinked like bears rousted out of hibernation. On a windowsill encrusted with white lime—or was it bird droppings?—three chickens with iridescent feathers and red wattles roosted like Japanese lanterns. Paul showed Simone a hole-in-the-wall shop, now defunct, its front window as blank as a flat-screen TV with the power off. "This was my favorite haunt as a teenager," he said. "It sold the tastiest potato chips in town. The owner scooped them fresh from the deep-fat fryer into paper bags. You had to eat them quick, while they were hot. Otherwise the grease congealed and the chips stuck to the paper."

"Sounds like you had a terrific childhood."

"Yeah, apart from pimples and indigestion."

"Come on, what's not to like?" She unknotted a scarf from her neck and wrapped it as a turban around her blowing hair.

On Gran Via, demonstrators blocked the street. In the Albaicín, where marchers stayed away from the steep hills, Paul seldom noticed the rallies that roiled downtown Granada—strikes for and against asylum seekers, unemployed laborers demanding jobs, old folks petitioning for higher pensions. Today's protesters waved banners calling for the Pacto del Olvido to be revoked. Paul explained, "When Franco died, the Fascists agreed to give up power in exchange for a Pact of Forgetting."

"Who is it who said that the first duty of memory is to forget?" Simone asked.

"A guilty person, I suspect."

They crossed into an ancient Arab silk market that had morphed into a tacky mall selling souvenirs. T-shirts stenciled with Arab calligraphy, anatomically correct dolls of naked baby Jesus, bullfight posters that read, "Your name here . . ."

"Getting back to your childhood," she said, "what didn't you like about it?"

"I was always at odds with my father."

"Always? There must have been some good times. What's the best one you remember?"

"What's your interest in my father?" This came out sharper than he intended.

"My interest is in you."

As they approached the biscuit-colored cathedral, they passed three priests who appeared to be reading their breviaries. But no, they were checking their cell phones.

"I'm waiting," Simone prompted him.

"The good times with my father were few and far between. But he did promise to bring me along on one of his secret missions when I got old enough. The summer I turned fifteen, we caught a commercial flight to Puerto Rico, then transferred to a seaplane piloted by a guy with an eye patch and a skull-and-crossbones tattoo.

"I was particularly susceptible to that sort of bullshit. I had just read *On the Road*, and I yearned to become the kind of man Kerouac described as 'mad to live, mad to talk, mad to be saved, desirous of everything at the same time, the ones who never yawn or say a commonplace thing but burn, burn, burn like fabulous Roman candles.'"

Simone released a peal of laughter. "I like you in this mood."

"Then you would have loved my father. He was one of Kerouac's fabulous Roman candles. Next to him, I was a fizzling bottle rocket. But on that trip it seemed possible I could become . . ."

"What?"

"A son he was proud of. A boy I was proud of."

They stopped at a Tunisian bakery and nibbled pink-and-green cookies, chewy and sweet as marzipan. "Sometimes you have to brush away honeybees before you bite into the pastry here."

"Stay on track," she said. "You were talking about your father."

"I thought I was talking about myself."

"That too."

Perched on tottering stools, they watched an electric cookie cutter carve out squares of dough and drop them on a grill. Paul was recounting how the seaplane had glided over a blue ocean sprinkled with gumdrop-green islands. His father recited their names as if they were family friends—Norman, Peter, Jost Van Dyke. As they descended toward an inlet, the seaplane's shadow rose up to meet them. Then they splashed down and skipped across sudsy water to a sun-bleached wharf. A pair of live hawksbill turtles lay there with their flippers trussed in front of them like hands in prayer.

"Do you really remember all this?" Simone broke in. "Or are you making it up?"

"Trust me, nothing's made up. With Dad, I was always half in the moment and half outside it, focusing very hard on the report Mom would demand of me. I didn't forget a thing."

They had landed someplace in the British Virgins, Paul said, on a barely inhabited spit of land. After the pilot docked the plane, they transferred to a Land Rover, and in growling low gear, they clattered up a mountain capped by what his father claimed was a rainforest. The pilot disputed that. By definition, he said, a rain forest needed a hundred inches of annual precipitation, far more than ever fell on the island.

"So sue me," his dad said. "So screw me."

At dead slow speed, they stuttered down the far side of the mountain through gullies of iron-smelling shale. Where the ground leveled off, a salt pond stank of sulfur, and beyond it, in a palm grove, the rotten-egg odor gave way to the smell of salt water.

"You either have a photographic memory or you're a great BS artist," Simone broke in again.

"I'm telling you what happened. You asked for my best memory of my father. This is it. There was a cove of white sand and a shack that had been slapped together out of driftwood and bamboo poles and palm fronds. After he dropped us and our supplies, the pilot drove back across the mountains."

"Leaving you and your father to play Robinson Crusoe," Simone said.

"I don't know what we were playing. Maybe just father and son. We hadn't had much practice at that. He acted as nervous as I was. He told me to go off and explore the cove."

"Maybe he sent you away so he could check on his assignment."

"Maybe. He had a shortwave radio in the shack."

"Your Boy's Own Adventure is fascinating," Simone said. "But this stool is putting my legs to sleep. Why don't we go someplace comfortable and have a glass of wine?"

At a bar down the block, Simone unwound the scarf from her hair and rewrapped it around her neck. The bartender set out a fresh plate of tapas. Her doubts about his pitch-perfect recall left

Paul self-conscious, and he hesitated to resume talking. But she urged him on.

He told her the ocean was bathtub temperature, the bottom white and smooth. He swam far out and rolled onto his back, buoyed by saltwater. "I wouldn't say I was completely happy," he admitted. "It was always hard being around Dad. But happiness seemed a glimmer on the horizon."

"Didn't it ever occur to you," Simone said, "that like a lot of kids of divorced parents, you were probably depressed? You should have talked to someone."

"Who?"

"Your prep school must have had a therapist."

"I had been raised not to discuss family matters. Now if you had been there"—he reached over and held her hand—"it would have been a piece of cake."

"Flattery will get you everywhere. Keep talking."

"One night the bugs got so bad, Dad had us stretch out in shallow water near the shore and spread handkerchiefs over our faces."

"I don't believe it. How could you sleep?"

"I didn't sleep. I was worried about sharks. Dad said he'd rather be eaten by a shark than stung to death by a billion mosquitoes."

"What about his mission? The secret assignment he promised to bring you on."

"I wondered when he'd get around to that. I asked, and he said first I had to learn how to handle a weapon. He owned a World War II German Luger that he bought off a guy who collected Nazi memorabilia. He showed me how to break it down and clean it. The tricky part was putting it back together. He made me practice until I got it right.

"We had a rubber dinghy. Dad insisted on doing all the rowing. He was still muscular and fit, no middle-aged spread on him. He had a full head of hair and a beard. He explained he kept his upper lip shaved so that a dive mask would stay sealed to it."

"Was he interested at all in your life?"

"He wasn't one for small talk. The only personal questions he asked were about my mother, and I avoided that subject. His favorite role was as an educator, not a father. He was hot to teach me how to spearfish. We went out in the dinghy, and he brought along masks and fins and snorkels and the Luger zipped into a waterproof bag."

"He brought a gun on a rubber boat?" she exclaimed.

"I was antsy about that myself. But I was already so worried about how I'd perform underwater, I didn't say a word. I listened to his instructions. He spit into his mask and scrubbed the lens. He rinsed his flippers in the sea so they'd slip onto his feet. He told me to do the same. Then he hoisted his rump up onto a side pontoon and cradled a speargun against his chest. I was on the opposite side, paying strict attention.

"'"The first rule,"' he said, '"is don't ever, and I mean never, take a cocked speargun on a boat. Wait until you're in the water before you trigger it. And stay to my left. I don't want to have to yank a spear out of your ass."'"

"Your father sounds like the drill sergeant in *Full Metal Jacket*."

"That's a pretty accurate picture. He handed me some twine and told me to tie it through the gills of the fish he shot. 'Careful of your fingers,' he said. 'Even little fish have teeth, and anything that has teeth will bite.'

"I couldn't help asking, 'What about sharks?'

"'Don't piss in your pants before we're even in the water. We won't see any sharks.'"

"'But what if we do?' I asked.

"'Stay behind me and stay cool. Don't try to outswim it, because, babycakes, you won't make it.' He yanked down his mask, clamped the snorkel between his teeth, and flipped back into the ocean. I followed him over the side, and right away, water rushed up my nose. Dad shoved my head back and cleared the mask. Then he dived."

"I asked about the best time with your father," Simone said. "This sounds like a nightmare."

"I'm getting to the good part. He used his speargun to point out angel fish, parrot fish, bonito, and amberjack. A school of tarpon swam by, and just for the hell of it, he squeezed the trigger and caught the caboose of the train broadside. The spear bounced off. The tarpon didn't even slow down. But a scale came loose, and Dad caught it and handed it to me like a gold doubloon from a pirate's chest."

They kept at it, Paul told her, for over an hour, diving, surfacing, and diving again. Each descent was like a tour of a submarine cathedral constructed of spirals and columns and flying buttresses of coral. The ocean streamed with different shades at different depths—aquamarine on the surface, darker as they dived down, pink when they encountered a mist of krill.

Eventually Peter Stewart quit pointing the speargun at fish and started shooting them. He skewered a fat, grumpy-looking grouper and a brace of yellowtail snapper. Paul strung them on the line and let their bloody quicksilver shapes flutter behind him.

"There was this feeling," he told Simone, "that my father and I had a flow, a rhythm, going on between us that had never been there before."

Paul sensed the same flow now between Simone and him, an oceanic connection. He was grateful that she had persuaded him to talk about his father, and he didn't want to stop. But he knew where this story was headed and didn't care to continue to the end. His voice trailed off.

Simone let a moment pass before she said, "What a beautiful father-and-son bonding experience."

He didn't contradict her. This didn't, in his opinion, constitute a lie. It was a narrator's selectivity—knowing when you've said enough and not too much. Simone didn't need to hear all of it—how a jagged outcropping of stag coral was steepled beneath them. From its shade rose a forbidding shape with the wingspan of a condor, a fierce triangular snout, black-and-white speckled fins and a barbed spike at its tail. When it torpedoed at them, Paul flung away the fish line and in panic tried to surface.

His father grabbed him and slapped the speargun at the leopard ray, chasing it off. For an instant, he looked like he might do the same thing to his son, slap him and chase him away. Instead, he dived after the string of fish Paul had dropped. A few fathoms down, they were twisting and writhing on the length of twine. But a barracuda beat him to the day's catch and shredded even those fish it didn't have time to devour.

Paul came up for air, his lungs on fire, the dive mask flattened painfully against his face. He tore it off and fought to breathe.

His father was already aboard the dinghy, seated between the oarlocks, the speargun clamped between his knees, like a suicide with a shotgun wedged under his chin. When Peter Stewart pried off his mask, a red circle framed his face. "You are such a fucking chickenshit," he raged. "A leopard ray doesn't even have teeth. Were you afraid it'd gum you to death?"

Paul clambered over the pontoon, and his father changed positions. Suddenly the speargun was aimed point-blank at his son. Too terrified to utter a sound, Paul processed what he saw and heard and felt in a scrambled sequence. The trigger clicked, his father shouted, the razor-sharp bolt seared Paul's cheek. He clapped a hand to the spot, expecting blood, but his palm came away clean.

It took both of them a moment to fathom what had happened. His father had brought the cocked speargun aboard the dinghy. When the trigger snapped, the spear burst out of its housing and broke the line, whipping Paul's cheek as it hurtled past and disappeared into the sea.

"That wasn't my fault," Peter Stewart said.

Paul couldn't speak.

"You made me so mad, I forgot to uncock it."

Paul still didn't speak.

"It could have killed you." His father sounded indignant rather than apologetic. "Don't act like a goddamn martyr. All you got is a rope burn."

Dizzied by the idiocy of events, Paul laughed. There seemed nothing else to do. His father laughed too and leaned into the oars, rowing them ashore. "Don't mention my little fuckup to your mother. Let this be our secret."

That night, with no fish to fry, they ate eggs, and because chickens on the island were fed fish scraps, the omelet Peter cooked tasted like rancid anchovies. Paul had trouble gagging down dinner. His father, however, ate and spoke with rare animation. Swigging a bottle of Johnny Walker Red, he abandoned his usual poker-face terseness and droned on and on, his voice as ceaseless as the whine of mosquitoes. Even after extinguishing the lanterns and stretching out on a cot beside his son, he continued drinking and talking.

Paul had seen his father tipsy before but never this drunk, never this voluble. He had heard him rant about women, but his father had never revealed so much about his tortured relationships. Scotch had loosened his tongue, and so, Paul guessed, had the shock of nearly killing his son.

As the drunken monologue dragged on, it came to him that his father had brought him to the island not just to test him and demonstrate his own masculine competence but to tell his side of a story that Paul had heard before exclusively from his mother and Virtudes.

Maundering on about Spain in the early '70s during the twilight of Franco's regime, Peter Stewart described his days as a Fulbright Fellow at the University of Granada. In that era, Spanish academics immediately suspected any American of being a CIA agent. It had stunned him that his colleagues bought into such a cliché. At the same time, he admitted, it flattered him. There were worse insults than being suspected of spying.

At the close of the fall semester, an attaché from the US Embassy invited him to lunch and encouraged Peter to keep his eyes and ears open. There were Fascists on campus determined to maintain Franco's legacy. The United States was also interested in the names of students and faculty who belonged to leftist groups. The attaché offered money, not much. Still, it supplemented Peter's paltry stipend and added to the ego trip of being an actor on a bigger stage.

Paul had never heard his father express guilt or apologize for anything. Now he confessed that, in incremental steps, he had been trapped in the role of a State Department puppet. After he returned to the States, he claimed he had no choice but to maintain a secret identity and keep filing reports.

He spoke about the breakdown of his marriage with the same candor as he discussed his clandestine activities. He was anxious for the boy to understand what it was like to be in bed with the US government and at the same time with a Spanish woman of a certain generation and class. He referred to her as a prisoner of concentric circles of repression and said that the *carmen* reminded him of a mausoleum or a morgue.

When his father began to lament his wife's sexual squeamishness, her icy resemblance to a statue of a saint on a tomb, Paul couldn't bear to go on listening. For the first time in his life, he screamed at his father to shut up. Rather than fight back, Peter Stewart plunked the empty Scotch bottle on the floor and didn't so much fall asleep as black out.

The next morning, Paul announced that he was leaving for home, and his father didn't argue for him to stay. He contacted the tattooed, one-eyed pilot over the shortwave, and they spent the rest of the day in the shack waiting for the Land Rover to rumble over the mountain through the faux rainforest. Each of them in his fashion nursed a horrendous hangover. Paul upchucked the previous night's fishy eggs, and his father swigged beer to settle his stomach. They had ample opportunity to talk, but neither of them said a word.

Decades later, in the bar where he and Simone finished their tapas and wine, Paul wondered whether it had been fear or wisdom that had kept him silent that last day on the island. He surmised that the same impulse kept him quiet now as Simone and he set off uphill through a huddle of lime-white houses where families sheltered like hermit crabs in beautiful conch shells.

CHAPTER VIII

In the following days, Simone suggested that they take Tahar out to dinner. "The hell with Spann and his orders. The guy is a control freak. I don't see why Tahar puts up with it."

"He's desperate for asylum in the States."

"But why treat him like a convict? He might as well be in solitary confinement."

Paul told her nothing about the fatwa and the danger Tahar ran if he were recognized in town. Nor did he mention the danger they ran being with him in public. "Talk to Tahar," he relented, "and see what he says."

Tahar needed no convincing. "I have been suffering *le cafard*." Despite using French slang for the blues, the dapper little Algerian sounded upbeat. "There will be no problem if I wear a disguise."

He put on baggy trousers and a loose-fitting brown sweater under a djellaba and a knit skullcap—a kufi, he called it—pulled low over his forehead. "Now I look like a poor Berber down from the mountains, agog at the big city."

They left the *carmen* in darkness, yet Paul feared that the mere glimpse of a white couple walking with an Arab would attract attention. To make things worse, Tahar stopped at a flower stand and bought a bouquet of chrysanthemums. He slipped one behind Simone's ear, then tried to do the same to Paul. When he refused, Tahar tucked the blossom into his skullcap.

"Jesus," Paul said, "chrysanthemums are flowers for the dead."

He steered them into back alleys where there were fewer pedestrians. Tahar remarked that the area reminded him of the casbah in Algiers. "Of course, the Albaicín is cleaner and in better repair. Walk anyplace in North Africa, and you'll understand why people are angry. They can't go anywhere without stumbling into a pothole or stepping in shit. Politicians boast about listening to the Arab street, but they behave like they've never been on one. Otherwise they'd collect the garbage and fix the potholes."

When they reached Plaza Bib Rambla, Tahar told them, "The name means sand gate. Muslims held jousting contests here. During the Reconquista, the Christians destroyed the Islamic library and burned all the books on this spot."

"Another proud moment in the history of religious tolerance," Simone drawled, the first sign that she was tiring of the professor's pedantry.

The evening paseo milled around the plaza, past outdoor bars and cafés whose tables were packed with drinkers. It was much too early for Andalusians to eat. Paul was anxious to move Tahar into a restaurant where there was less danger of his being spotted. But a bossy waiter suggested that they sit outside under a lamp that blasted Saharan heat. Paul insisted on a table inside, away from the front window. The waiter maintained that all those tables were reserved.

"Paul, you take Mr. Spann's worries too seriously," Tahar said. "He takes himself too seriously."

Paul signaled for him to hold his voice down. Tahar ignored the warning. Then the plate glass rattled behind his head. They all whirled around. A Black man was pounding the glass, gesturing and wailing. Paul's instant fear was that some random refugee, a beggar swaddled in a filthy blanket, had recognized Tahar. Then he realized that it was Blessed.

"Who is it?" Tahar asked in alarm.

"A man who used to work for me."

"Why's he so upset? The waiter should have a word with him."

"Or call the police," Simone said.

"No, we don't want the police," Tahar said.

"I'll take care of this." Paul motioned for Blessed to meet him outside. His blanket was rank and crusted with grime. Paul urged him toward Bib Rambla's central fountain. Blessed pushed back, seizing him by the shoulders and shaking him. Words and saliva sprayed between his teeth. "He steal my job."

A crowd gathered, expecting a fight, rooting for a fight. People yelled for Paul to flatten the stinking *negrito.* Blessed's tongue fumbled with foreign words. "Patsy tells me," he shouted.

"Calm down. Don't make trouble."

They stood chest to chest. Blessed's breath was foul. Mud flecks scrawled a message in a mysterious alphabet across his chest. "Patsy tells me," he shouted again.

"Patsy's wrong. Tahar didn't steal your job. He's writing a book."

Blessed fell back a step. "Who cleans?"

"Patsy."

"Why not me?"

"Not now."

"When?"

"When business is better."

"How will you find me? I live in a box."

Pierced by sadness, Paul pictured him sleeping in a cardboard carton. "When the time's right, I'll look for you."

Paul pulled fifty euros from his pocket and handed them over. Tears streamed down Blessed's gaunt cheeks, not in gratitude, Paul knew, but in an outrage as palpable and pungent as his unwashed body. He had lost so much weight, he might have been a funerary doll carved out of burned wood. The paseo whirled him away before either of them could say more.

Back at the table, Simone and Tahar were holding hands. He might have been reading her palm; she was examining his missing fingernails. They were comparing their disfigurement—hers caused by turpentine, his by torture.

Simone glanced up at Paul. "What was that about?"

"He was hungry and needed a handout."

"Sad," Tahar said. "Islam once brought refinement, spices, gold, and sumptuous pleasure to Granada. Now it brings refugees and disease."

CHAPTER IX

Simone Pierce summoned to Tahar's mind the women he used to gaze at from a distance as a university student in Oran. Among the Algerian coeds, all members of a privileged class, there had been a number of French girls. Back before the Islamic crackdown, they smoked and drank wine together in sidewalk cafés. They flaunted their bare arms and legs, their uncovered hair. They wore dresses so gauzy the outline of their underpants showed through. They sunbathed during the day in bikinis at Plage les Andalouses and danced at night in discos along the Corniche. Their easy availability—or so his more adventurous classmates bragged—was something Tahar was too shy to test.

Later, from the sophisticated perspective of Oxford, this had struck him as ridiculous. The behavior of North African boys lacked suavity. Tahar emulated the droll indifference of British men, who proved that the more you ignored a woman, the more likely she was to desire you.

Not that Tahar had had much sexual experience. English coeds held little appeal for him. Pale even in summer, buttoned up in winter under layers of wool, wary in all seasons of foreign students with swarthy complexions, they weren't worth the risk of making a fool of himself.

Simone presented an altogether more alluring package. Beautiful, outgoing, intelligent, thrillingly like the actresses that Tahar had fallen in love with in American films. She had a habit of touching you as she talked and flirtatiously shaking back her hair. With the haughty waiter at the restaurant, she had insisted on sending her main dish back to be reheated. This impressed Tahar, who wasn't accustomed to women asserting themselves.

After the run-in with the Black beggar, Paul had fallen quiet at the restaurant, and Tahar had filled the silence. He spoke to Simone as if she were a student in his classroom, the only one paying attention. On the hike back to the *carmen*, Paul was clearly preoccupied. Still, Tahar expected him to pair off with Simone once they arrived, leaving him to retreat alone to his room. But then Paul said he had emails to answer, wished them good night, and headed for his tower.

In bewilderment, Simone said to Tahar, "You haven't seen my work."

"No. Unfortunately not."

"Like to come in?"

"If it's not too late."

"I'm a night owl." She unlocked the door.

"I'll get rid of my costume." In her studio, he removed his skullcap and djellaba. "A fascinating chap, Paul. I can't help thinking of him as a Mozarab."

"A what?"

"A figure from Granada's early history. A Christian who remained during the Islamic occupation, speaking Arabic and following local customs yet secretly clinging to his beliefs."

"Yes, he's a mystery man. He keeps his beliefs to himself."

Oxford had shaped Tahar's artistic taste and his critical vocabulary. Among the donnish affectations he had adopted was clasping his hands behind his back and postponing any opinion until he had mulled things over. As he strolled past a series of meticulously rendered penises, he maintained a pretense of sangfroid. All the while, he suffered the tumbling sensation of being slammed back into his cell and humiliated. He remembered the stick figures etched in blood on the walls. Desire, and the anxiety that inevitably accompanied it, closed on him like a claw.

"Extraordinary." He breathed. "Transfixing."

Simone moved disconcertingly close as he praised her work.

"I'm impressed by the brushwork, the sinuousness of line. Would it be entirely off the mark," he asked, "to note the influence of Lucian Freud? I'm guessing there's also a debt to Francis Bacon in the distorted postures of your models."

"You're putting me in flattering company," she said.

Coming to the canvas of a vagina, he felt speechless—which was precisely why he made himself talk. Language was his only defense, a flimsy shield against inexpressible regret. Confronted by what he had lost and feared he'd never regain, he polished his praise to meaningless perfection.

"What I admire most is the balance, the tension, you create between clinical realism and surrealistic touches of humor. The green sprig of pubic hair is priceless. Of course your art could never be exhibited in my country. Artists are censored at the same time as we're bombarded on TV by pornographic images."

"These are Algerian programs?" she asked.

"Who knows where they originate? They reach Algeria by satellite. During the Islamist insurrection, imams condemned satellite dishes. *Paraboliques diaboliques*, they called them. If you were caught with one on your roof, you could have your throat slit. But that didn't deter people."

"Sex is a powerful force," she said. "You can't legislate—"

"A potentially revolutionary force," he broke in. "In Muslim society, we suffer what Ernst Bloch described as 'the simultaneity of the non-simultaneous.'"

"I'm afraid you've lost me."

"The mixture of archaic cultural patterns with modern global elements. In Algeria, for instance, some tribes continue to practice female circumcision to thwart sexual pleasure while at the same time orgies are broadcast on TV. You can't blame people for being confused."

"About what?"

He couldn't guess whether she was genuinely interested or goading him on with disingenuous questions. "Sex," he said. "Men see it on satellite TV but realize they can't have it unless they're married. And they can't marry because they can't find jobs. This drives them to violence."

"Then they blame women."

"Exactly. But they blame politicians too, and they . . . and they . . ." Trapped between Simone, this fragrant American woman, and the image of spread thighs, he lost track of what he meant to say.

"I love talking to you," Simone said. "I'd like to paint you and continue the conversation."

"Now? Tonight?"

"No. When we have more time and better light."

"Paint me how?"

"With a brush, silly."

"With clothes? Or without?"

"My specialty is nude life studies."

Tahar laughed a quiet, ironic laugh, like a debonair actor in a romantic comedy. "Your invitation honors me. But I'm not the model you want."

"You have no idea what I want." Her voice was soft, seductive, her eyes mineral hard.

"Sorry, *chérie*, I'm not the man." Carrying on in the role of continental charmer, he kissed her hand, then left before he completely unraveled.

In his room, he removed his trousers and underpants and hastened into the bathroom. His groin throbbed—in distress more than desire. He splashed cold water on himself, and the release of tension—the relief of pain—left him weak-kneed. If Simone could see him now, she would recoil in disgust. Unlike the proud cocks she painted, his was a cruel joke, a smutty cartoon. When erect, his penis curved to the left, then curled back on itself like a question mark.

He had consulted doctors in Tlemcen, Oran, and Algiers. All of them diagnosed Peyronie's disease caused by extensive calcifying scar tissue. Had he been in an accident? they asked. How had he suffered such traumatic damage to his genitals?

When he told them he had been tortured, they asked no follow-up questions. If Tahar was a common criminal who had been abused during police interrogation, the doctors didn't want to know. And if he told them the truth, that terrorists had done this to him, it would be all the more urgent to concentrate on his symptoms and ignore the causes. No sane person dared to be at cross-purposes with the country's radical groups.

The medical consensus was that Tahar's condition might remedy itself in six months or a year. When his symptoms didn't improve, doctors prescribed topical creams and steroid injections. Finally they administered shock-wave therapy and traction, using devices that Tahar's torturers might have designed. Nothing helped.

In the end, doctors advised surgery but suggested that he seek treatment overseas. The United States had the most reliable surgeons and the best outcomes. The difficulty was obtaining a visa from the Americans and permission to travel from the Algerians. Then there was the cost.

In the end, Tahar had contacted the US Embassy in Madrid rather than the one in Algiers, where US officials barricaded themselves inside bombproof buildings. Convinced that his emails would be intercepted and phone calls tapped, he dispatched typewritten letters to Spain by international courier service. Bill Spann eventually answered, and now everything depended on the novel Tahar was supposed to be finishing and the information it provided about Islamic fundamentalists.

As the pain diminished along with his desire, anger took possession of Tahar. Anger and shame. Simone had humiliated him. Now he longed to humiliate her, hurt her. Much as she might maintain that she as a woman was marginalized by the hegemony of men, she hadn't a clue what it was like to be shunted aside, to feel that nobody could bear to look at you or touch you.

His anger gradually guttered out, and Tahar no longer felt like punishing Simone. He only wanted to talk to her. Wracked by a loneliness powerful enough to pulverize his bones, he resisted the urge to rush to her room right away and apologize. She had said she'd like to continue their conversation while she painted him. Why not serve as her mentor, which after all was another word for model?

CHAPTER X

More for distraction than to check email, Paul powered up the computer. The guilt roused by the run-in with Blessed had sunk talons impossible to pry out. For weeks, everywhere he went, every homeless person he passed reminded him of the great wrong he had done.

He focused on deleting spam and responding to inquiries from applicants. He told them the *carmen* had no vacancies and suggested they reapply later. Given what Spann paid him, he felt no financial pressure. But Simone was a worry looming over his life. He had no idea how it would end. Would she leave or stay? And if she stayed, what then?

Now she was downstairs, with Tahar for a late-night private studio visit. With his British airs and French aplomb, Tahar wasn't apt to be perturbed by nude paintings. The test would come when she asked him to pose for her.

That would also be the test for Paul. He didn't regard himself as the jealous type. The hallmark of his arts residency was a tolerance for fluid relationships. But the intensity of his attachment to

Simone—his possessiveness, to be honest—caught him off guard. He didn't like to envision her, even fully clothed and professionally detached, sketching the naked Algerian.

Paul shut down the computer and undressed for bed, buffeted by uncomfortable emotions and by cold air rifling through the poorly sealed windows. He listened to the wind rise, bearing tatters of flamenco music from the Gypsy caves in Sacramonte. Strangely, the heel-stomping dances were less audible than the anguished laments over lost love. Duende seized Paul. Sadness, soulfulness.

The windows blurred in an abrupt rain squall. He might have been at sea, in a ship's cabin, squinting blindly through portholes. The rain fell harder and drowned the flamenco music but not the duende. The *saudade*, as Patsy would put it in Portuguese. Every language had a word for sadness. Paul couldn't recall the Arabic term for what Blessed must be suffering—grief at his isolation from Allah and everything else.

Wraithlike at the restaurant window, Blessed had resembled a phantasm risen from a grave. When Paul touched him, his bones were skeletal, his voice haunted. How could Paul ever hope to find him.

He hated Bill Spann—no, he hated himself—for throwing Blessed out. That he had done it for money and to please Simone deepened to his desolation.

• • •

In the morning, he skipped breakfast, both to delay facing Tahar and Simone and to consider how to help Blessed. At noon, he didn't anticipate finding anybody in the kitchen, but Patsy was there tidying up, or pretending to.

"The foreign whore is fucking the Arab," she flung at him.

"I told you not to call her that. And I won't stand for your talking to me in that tone."

"How should I talk in a house full of *sinverguenzas*, shameless ones? Cleaning her room, I found his *touca*." She used Portuguese slang for "cap" as well as "condom."

"He was looking at her paintings."

"Her paintings!" She let out a lip fart.

"I never thought of you as the sanctimonious type," Paul said.

"I'm the type that doesn't care to be around a woman who behaves like she has a lizard squirming between her legs. I'm the type that doesn't fancy watching her boss act like a fool."

"Are you bitching because you have to clean her room?"

"I'm bitching because I see you losing your head over a woman and letting business go to hell."

"I appreciate your concern," he said wearily.

"My biggest worry is over this Arab. He should leave and Blessed should come back. The other day, I bumped into Blessed begging in the market. He looked like a dog ready to be put down."

"Did you tell him about Tahar?"

"Tell him what?"

"Tell him anything?"

"Blessed is not easy to talk with."

"But did you mention Tahar?" Paul demanded.

"I mentioned we now have an Arab here along with the whore. Excuse me, the lady artist."

"If you run into him again, find out where he lives. I need to know how to reach him. And give him this." He handed her a fistful of euros.

• • •

When Bill Spann showed up for his weekly session with Tahar, he told Paul, "We gotta talk. Not in here. Outside."

Freezing gusts scoured Huerta de Carlos, blasting sand across the stone paving as they headed for the gym equipment. Bundled up in a ski parka and amply padded with fat, Spann moved awkwardly, his hulking size and ragged breath creating the illusion of speed. He lowered his bulk onto the exercise bike, cupped his hands to his mouth, and touched a match to a cigarette.

"Tahar tells me you all had dinner in town." Spann pedaled and pumped the handlebars, puffing smoke like a steam locomotive. "One happy little family."

Paul didn't get why Tahar had revealed this. "So what?" he managed to say.

"So are you out of your fucking mind?"

"He's been moping around, bitching about having shack fever. He paces in the courtyard like a prisoner counting steps."

"I warned you somebody sure as hell would recognize him."

"It was Blessed who recognized me, not Tahar."

"It could have been a hit man. Or some local goofball who read about the fatwa online and got it in his head to take Tahar out."

"But it wasn't. It was the poor bastard you made me fire."

"I *made* you?" Spann hooted with laughter. "I dangled the

money, and you jumped at it. And let's not forget, we still don't have a clue who Blessed really is."

"I'll tell you who he is. He's too weak and hungry now to hurt anybody."

"All this sympathy for the underdog, you're breaking my heart. Look, I'm working for a president who's got no patience for refugees from shithole countries. Get with the goddamn program."

"I'm running an arts residency, not a concentration camp."

"Tahar can walk away anytime he wants to. So can you. But then it's bye-bye asylum for him. And bye-bye for you too."

"Are you threatening me?"

"What if I am?"

Paul felt an overpowering urge to knock him off the exercise bike. But he knew that Spann would bounce back up and smash him.

Spann dismounted and plucked at the trousers wadded in his crotch. "I'm leaving the country for the next couple of weeks. In an emergency, I need to know I can count on you. If you have an iota of self-preservation, you better remember the US has some nasty laws against aiding terrorists."

"Are you telling me now that Tahar is a terrorist?"

"I'm not telling you anything of the sort. I'm just saying you need to show better judgment. In case of trouble, you can contact me through the embassy. In the meantime, no more happy meals downtown."

• • •

That night, Paul didn't wait to be invited. He declared that he wanted Simone.

"Now there's a nice idea." She swung the door to her room wide. "How shall we celebrate our reunion?"

He took her in his arms, sliding his hand down the deep groove of her spine under the waistband of her jeans. He didn't allow her to disappear into the bathroom to undress. He removed her clothes with the urgency of an ER surgeon. Smiling, she whispered, "Whoa."

He didn't slow down. He picked her up and placed her in bed on her hands and knees. Her spine arched, then curled, and arched again. He marveled at how perfectly they fitted. A vulgarity from his adolescence popped into his head, the Gypsy's curse—"May you find a cunt that fits." Paul had found his.

Afterward, Simone drew the duvet up over them. "It's cold." Rolling onto her side, she held him in her hand as if to warm him. "Did your mother teach you about sex?"

"She was educated in a convent. After her divorce, I doubt she ever permitted herself to think about sleeping with a man."

"So it was your father who taught you?"

"What's this thing you have about my father?"

"You're the one who has a thing about your father. I have a thing about you."

"Maybe he imagined he taught me by example. The only actual advice he offered was 'Remember, it'll stretch a yard before it tears an inch.'"

"I assume he was referring to a penis."

"You're funny, you know that?"

"I have my moments."

"What was Tahar's reaction to your painting?"

"Caution. He didn't commit himself to anything you wouldn't expect from a Frenchified intellectual."

"That covers a lot of ground. Did you ask him to pose?"

"Of course. If you can't have the one you love, ask the one you're with. He said he wasn't what I'm looking for."

"What do you make of that?"

"You always wonder: Is he not hung? Or is he hung up?"

"Patsy thinks you're fucking Tahar."

"What a toxic little package she is. Didn't it ever occur to you to get rid of her?"

"Are you volunteering to do the cleaning and cooking?"

"Seriously, you should hire somebody less nosy and obnoxious."

"Okay, seriously. Patsy has an EU passport and has worked here for years. That gives her rights. I'd have labor unions picketing the *carmen* around the clock."

"You got rid of Blessed," Simone said.

"That's different—apples and oranges. Apples and an entirely different food group. Legally, he was never an employee. Legally, he has no right to be in Spain."

She snuggled close and kissed his ear. "I realize you hated to fire him. I'm grateful you did it for me. He scared the hell out of me the other night."

Paul sagged back on the pillow. "What scared me is how awful he looked after living on the street."

"What a sweetie you are." She rolled on top of him, clamping him tight between her thighs. "Your mother may not have taught you about the birds and the bees, but she sure taught you guilt."

"It's not guilt I feel. It's . . . okay, it is guilt. But it's also the unfairness that bothers me. Here we are rattling around in a huge *carmen* while he's living in a cardboard box."

"Such a caring Catholic boy," she said. "I bet you've never done anything wrong in your life."

"I've done my share."

"Tell me about it." Her tone, its teasing lilt, spread a heat in him that was half anger, half arousal. "Tell me the worst thing you've ever done."

"What's this, confession? 'Bless me, Father, for I have sinned'?"

He considered describing the boy drowning in the river. The kid whose death still plagued him. Instead, he blurted, "I fucked my father's wife."

She peeled off him so abruptly there was a moist pop. "Your mother?"

"God, no, his third wife. Or was it his fourth? I lose track."

"You've got to tell me."

"I just told you."

"You have to tell me everything. How? Where? When?"

"I have to? What are you? Homeland Security?"

"I wish you'd tell me." She softened her voice. "Really, Pablo, I'm dying to hear."

"I've never told anybody."

"All the more reason to tell me. It'll be our secret."

"Every time I flew to Florida," he said, "my father had a different woman in the house. My junior year in college, he was shacked up with Dale, one of his grad students. Standard procedure for him. She was attractive and intelligent and personable. Again, standard."

"Your father must have been a very charismatic man."

"His charisma missed me. I regarded his sex life as an embarrassment. Dale started needling him about getting old. She suggested the two of us go out dancing since he was too tired."

"Sounds like she was trying to spice things up," Simone said.

"It worried me, her sassiness. I'd seen what he was capable of when someone crossed him. The next year, over spring vacation, Dale and he were still together, but now they were married, and somehow she was in a wheelchair."

"'Somehow'? You didn't ask?"

"Of course I asked. Dad told me Dale would explain if she cared to. But she never said a word about it, never gave the slightest indication she welcomed questions."

"Maybe she was afraid to admit what happened."

"She didn't appear to be afraid of anything. The house had been refitted with ramps and grab bars, and she rolled around discussing her dissertation. She meant to finish it, she said, and have a teaching career. She swore not to let anything hold her back. Her wheelchair, I remember, had an ashtray on one arm and a holder for a cocktail glass on the other. She smoked and drank, and we talked about everything except her marriage and her health. You'd never know anything was wrong with her unless you looked at her feet. They were shriveled, child size. Sometimes she asked me to help her with assisted coughing."

"What's that?" Simone said.

"She couldn't keep her lungs clean on her own. So she showed me what to do." Paul demonstrated on Simone, clamping his palms around her rib cage, then slowly tightening his grip. Like a caged bird, Simone's heart beat under fragile bones.

"Did you ever think that your father had hurt her? Crippled her?"

"From what I knew of his temper and his drinking, I had my suspicions."

"You make him sound like a monster."

"You asked me the worst thing I ever did. Not the worst Dad did. Do you want to hear this or not?"

"Of course, go on. Don't be upset."

"Well, it's an upsetting subject." He paused, hoping Simone would signal for him to stop. She didn't. "Dale liked to swim in the ocean. She said salt water kept her flexible and eased her pain. Dad was too busy with his classes to drive her to the beach. So I drove. Sometimes we'd head east to the Atlantic, sometimes west to the Gulf coast. In either direction, the trip was only an hour.

"She said to me, 'Your father treats me like I'm broken. I'm not. I just can't walk.' At the beach, I carried her into the water. 'You don't have to hold me,' she said. 'I can swim.' And I said, 'What if I like holding you?' She laughed. 'Remember all the guns in your father's bureau.'"

"You two were begging for trouble."

"I felt sorry for her. But she never seemed to feel sorry for herself. She insisted on swimming alone while I waited on the beach. Then when she got tired, she came out of the ocean on her own."

"Came out how?"

"She dog-paddled to the shore and crawled over the sand, dragging her legs behind her. It broke my heart to watch that. She looked like someone in a sadistic cartoon, a shipwreck survivor on a desert island. The only thing missing was a caption that made sense of it.

"One time we stayed on after dark. When the other people left, Dale wanted to swim again, and I cradled her to my chest." He took Simone in his arms. "This time I didn't turn her loose. I kept ahold of her, and we drifted into deeper water full of phosphorescence. It glowed on our skin. She rubbed her hands over me, like she was scrubbing it away, and I did the same to her. You can guess where it went from there."

"I don't get it." Simone's breath was warm on his chest, just as Dale's had been. "You were supposed to tell me the worst thing you ever did. Where's the bad part? You didn't force her, did you?"

"No, but I knew it was wrong."

"Your mother would be proud of you. Still an altar boy after all these years."

"I knew right away that nothing good could come of it."

"Maybe it was good for her. Ever think of that?"

"I guess not. Anyway, we didn't do it again. We steered clear of each other the rest of my visit. I was afraid Dad would find out. Much later, after I graduated and moved back to Granada, he wrote me—he didn't call, he didn't telegram or email—he sent a letter that she was dead. It took ten days to get to me. Much too late to fly back for the funeral."

"Please don't tell me you blamed yourself."

"Not really. I assumed whatever crippled her had finally killed her. But I always wondered whether Dale told him I fucked her."

"You made love to her," Simone corrected him.

"Whatever. Then he died, and weeks after he was buried, I read his obituary online."

"It must have been devastating to learn he killed himself."

Paul raised his head. "How'd you know?"

"You mentioned it."

"I don't remember that."

"Maybe all your talk about his pistols and his crazy behavior made me think it."

"Yeah, maybe." He settled back.

"Did it shock you that he committed suicide?"

"I was always afraid he'd kill somebody else, not himself. Now it's your turn. What's the worst thing you ever did?"

"You don't want to know."

She was right. He really didn't have it in him for more talk.

"I will tell you one thing, though," she said. "It's not the worst thing; still, I've kept it secret."

"I'm all ears."

"One semester in college, I decided to become trisexual? As in I'd try anything. A lot of the other girls in the dorm were doing it. My roommate and I experimented at being lipstick lesbians."

"How long did that last?" he asked.

"Like I said—a semester."

"What ended it?

"Would it worry you if it didn't end?"

"Consenting adults," he said.

"How enlightened and liberal. To tell you the truth, I got tired of pretending I liked the taste of pussy."

CHAPTER XI

Blessed roamed Bib Rambla. Everywhere he moved, the crowd gave ground, isolating him on the island of his own sour flesh. At each step, he stood in a well of stink, a ferocious figure with wild eyes and wilder hair. His first thought was to wait for Paul, Simone, and Tahar to finish dinner, then follow them down a dark alley. He couldn't decide who to attack first, who he hated most. The lady artist? The Arab? His former boss, the liar who had kicked him out of the *carmen*?

But he noticed the Guardia Civil patrolling the plaza, one pair on foot, their flat black patent-leather hats gleaming in lamplight. A second pair straddled motorcycles, armored in crash helmets, white leather gloves gripping handlebars. This was no place to settle a score.

Blessed flowed with the swell of pedestrians surfing past shop windows glittering with unimaginable luxuries—gold watches, diamond necklaces, crystal vases. Any one of these treasures could rescue him, but as in a nightmare, they remained just out of reach.

Blessed didn't know the day of the week, much less the month. But his hunger reminded him of Ramadan, the Islamic period of fasting. Only now there was no iftar feast each day after sundown.

His quest for food was constant. At the rear doors of restaurants, where refugees lucky enough to land menial jobs packed garbage into plastic bags, he had become a familiar figure, a pet. Workers fed him discarded bread and leftover food from dinner tables. At a seafood place, a simpatico South American gave him fish heads. At first, Blessed flinched in disgust. But the fellow showed him how to gnaw a tuna head, teasing out bits of brain and the eyeballs with his tongue. Blessed did the same, and when the South American turned his back, he stole a sharp scaling knife and concealed it under his blanket.

Then he trudged toward the outskirts of Granada, far from the historical center to the city's grubby fringes. The night seemed to somersault; light soared up from the sidewalk, darkness plummeted from the sky. In a bleak zone of factories and warehouses, most streetlights had been struck blind by stones. One globed lamp had survived intact, and boys kicked around a ball under the humming cone of light.

Blessed had played soccer barefoot on the wind-scoured fields of his village. He remembered the heat, the exhilaration. But this game had no apparent goal, no rules. Random and frantic as insects, the boys appeared to be fighting, not playing. When they spotted Blessed, they shouted insults and obscenities. They closed in around him and demanded money. Reaching under his blanket as if for a wallet, he pulled out the knife. He didn't need to use it. Showing it was enough to back them off.

Blessed had told Paul that he lived in a box for furniture. But when the self-storage unit had started to smell like him, the manager had thrown him out. He'd moved to a new spot where the owner believed that a ragged Black man might be better than a vicious dog at frightening off robbers. A guard dog had to be fed. Blessed didn't.

A hut stood in an abandoned quarry at the bottom of a steep depression banked by mounds of rubble. Blessed slithered down to it on a muddy path. Then, plodding along as if in wooden clogs, he stumbled across an expanse of rock tailings, an immense puzzle of missing and broken pieces.

A giant rotary saw presided over this mineral waste. The owner, who rarely came around, maintained that the saw was valuable and would someday be sold for scrap metal. Blessed's job was to prevent thieves from swiping the great wheel, many of whose teeth were ruined by rust.

In exchange, he got to live in a hut where tools used to be stored. Constructed of stone, it had rock walls, a rock floor and roof, a rock chair, and a rock bench for a bed. In this season, the stones radiated piercing cold, and tufts of damp moss drooled from cracks in the ceiling.

The Koran promised that "in the alternation of night and day, and in all Allah has created in the heavens and the earth, there are signs for righteous men." Blessed searched for these signs. He prayed for them. But they were no place to be found in this world, where he was the only animate object. Stretched out on his stone bed, he felt he was moving. He was silent yet heard voices. Was Allah whispering to him? Or were criminals plotting to steal the saw? Night air streamed through his emaciated body as if through a window screen.

He remembered the snake he had beheaded in the garden, and this brought back images of decapitated prisoners in video reels of victims bleeding out in the desert. He wondered whether his scaling knife was sharp enough to cut off a man's head. He tested the blade against his thumb and sliced open the skin. He sucked the blood as a baby would milk from his mother's breast.

Lighting a kerosene lantern, Blessed was careful not to rip the mantle as he touched a match to it. The flame caught with a whoosh, and soft light lacquered the stone walls. He dropped to his knees, pressed his head to the cold floor, and begged for strength. "I seek refuge from the mischief of the slinking prompter who whispers in the hearts of men."

Outside the hut, rain fell like the judgment of God. Forked tongues of lightning flashed over the sky; fiery rings of water spread across the rocks. Then thunder brought back the darkness.

Blessed slept and dreamed of sneaking into the *carmen* and killing the artist lady. Because of what she painted, she deserved to die. But when he woke, he realized he couldn't in conscience kill her unless he killed himself at the same time, trading his life for her death. Martyrdom was the moral solution, he thought, suicide his salvation.

• • •

A lake pooled around the hut, glittering under the risen sun like cracked glass. He washed his face and brushed his teeth with the *miswah.* The Prophet decreed that cleanliness was half of faith. But what if the water was polluted? How could it clean him? These dilemmas nagged him. Still, he took the water into his mouth and snorted it through his nostrils.

En route to the city, he paused under the arc light where the boys had kicked a ball around the night before. He wondered whether he had dreamed that ugly incident. Now, in the harsh glare of parked cars, his eyes glazed over, and he questioned whether he had the courage to kill anyone.

With what remained of Paul's money, he had planned to buy bread and coffee. Instead, he stopped at an Internet café, where the cashier complained that Blessed stank. Yet he quit quibbling when Blessed paid ten euros for computer time.

Lottery tickets and sunflower seeds carpeted the floor, and tissues slimy with snot or something worse stuck to Blessed's shoes. The screens he passed appeared to display the aftermath of a terrorist attack. Bodies and body parts lay tangled together, oozing fluid. He reached an empty chair in the back row before he realized everybody else had logged on to porn sites.

It seemed to him that the computer keys didn't respond to the pressure of his fingertips. It was more as if the machine pulled him from website to website. He pecked out the name and address of the *carmen*, and under a tab for Current Residents, Simone Pierce's name flashed into view.

If, as Paul claimed, the Arab was there writing a book, why wasn't he listed? The last time Blessed and Patsy had crossed paths in the market, she had given him the Algerian's name printed on a scrap of paper.

Blessed typed it now and searched Arabic websites, scrolling until he discovered a match—a professor at the university in Tlemcen. A summary of his publications in Arabic and French filled three pages, ending with footnotes about Derrida, Barthes, and Lacan. Blessed attempted to read them and realized this writing wasn't for him. He couldn't guess who it was for.

In a newspaper article about Tahar, a Salafist imam denounced him as an apostate, a blasphemer. Declaring a fatwa against him, the imam commanded Believers to hunt him down and feed his body to dogs. Because he had maligned the faith, he wasn't worthy of having his corpse washed and buried in a Muslim cemetery. In the name of Allah, the Compassionate, the Merciful, the imam condemned Tahar to death. "Well oh well has he deserved this doom," the fatwa concluded.

The desire to kill them all seized Blessed. First, the lady artist, then Mahmoud, then Paul. There was nothing else for him on this earth. No other path to paradise. With one act, he could redeem his sinful life. He pictured coaxing them into the confined space of the kitchen, where, strapped into a suicide vest studded with bolts and ball bearings, he would slaughter everybody.

Blessed keyed in the website where he had previously read about bomb-making. To produce TATP explosive powder, you needed hydrogen peroxide and sulfuric acid. A triggering device wasn't necessary. Friction or heat could set off the explosion.

The computer screen blinked once, then went blank. The cashier called out, "You can't just sit there. Pay for more time or make room for the next customer."

Blessed glanced around. No customers were waiting. He begged for a few extra minutes. But the cashier refused, and Blessed didn't dare argue and give the guy an excuse to call the cops. Shrouded in his blanket, he headed for the door.

He swayed as he walked—first toward the town center, then back toward the rock quarry. He needed food, and he needed to think. The two warred within his head, and he had to sit down. At a bus stop, he slumped onto a metal bench, squeezing into a corner where clear plastic walls propped him upright. He yearned to shut his eyes and sleep. But to stop moving was already a risk. To lie down was to surrender to despair. The Guardia Civil was sure to grab him.

He ran through what he had read about bomb-making. The computer promised that all the materials were available in the average house. But he didn't live in an average house. He lived in a stone hut and owned nothing except a knife and spare clothes. He had no money for sulfuric acid and hydrogen peroxide. Even if he succeeded in stealing bomb-making materials, how could he build a bomb in the stone hut? He had barely enough strength to walk there empty-handed. How could he clamber out of the quarry in a suicide vest? He was bound to blow himself up, dying for nothing, his skull firing like a cannonball from the tube of his neck, his body reduced to a smudge on the mounds of rubble.

His strength ebbed, and his thoughts scattered. Blessed curled his knees to his chest and closed his eyes. The transparent walls of the bus shelter magnified the sun's heat; he feared he was burning. He prayed to be arrested, he prayed to be deported, he prayed to die. How had he ever believed that he had the courage to become a martyr?

Blessed slept and dreamed wisdom from the Book. Allah was as close to him now as the vein in his neck. It came to him that he didn't have to kill Tahar, Simone, Paul, and himself to win salvation.

He pushed to a seated position, opened his eyes, and spotted a path. Paul was in mortal danger, as was everyone else at the *carmen*. An assassin need not travel from North Africa. A fundamentalist from Little Morocco could easily climb the staircases of the Albaicín and break into the residency and slaughter everybody. But if Blessed warned Paul of the danger, he might be welcomed back.

Blessed pushed to his feet, and the ground quaked under him. Walking was like falling. Pitching forward and catching himself before he hit the pavement, he floundered in the direction of the quarry, intending to hide in the hut and make a plan.

CHAPTER XII

Tahar tapped his fingertips on Simone's door. When that prompted no reply, he rapped his knuckles, and a voice, obviously annoyed, answered, "I'm working."

"I'm here to work with you."

The bolt slid back, and the hefty wooden door swung wide of its own weight. Simone clutched a rag in one hand. Balled into a fist, the other hand was jammed against her hip. She wore a blue NYPD sweatshirt and a pair of spattered jeans. The shapeless shirt and tight denims gave her a tough, mannish look, an androgyny that appealed to Tahar.

"You invited me to pose," he reminded her.

Her impatience evaporated; the corners of her eyes crinkled in a smile. He stepped into the room, and she locked the door behind him.

"Concerned about security?"

"I value my privacy," she said.

"Considering your subject matter, that's wise." He affected the jolly, avuncular tone that he assumed with students. "The *carmen* is constructed like a prison. But I think the bars are mostly window dressing."

On the desk, a computer screen displayed a naked man lolling on a bed. Because of a faulty connection, the bed shimmered like a turquoise pool of water, and the man appeared to be drowning, his body arched in a paroxysm of pain or pleasure. Before Tahar could guess whether this was a live feed or a screen saver, Simone cut the power.

"I imagine the *carmen*'s original owner," Tahar said, "installed the grillwork to protect his family. But there's really no such thing as a safe house."

Simone was scrubbing paint off her hands with a rag soaked in fingernail-polish remover. "You can undress in the bathroom if you like."

"Is that what your other models do?"

"When I log on to Chat Random, they're already naked."

"I have no objection to undressing in front of you."

"Whatever floats your boat."

He unbuttoned and unbuckled while she sorted through her brushes. "What floats your boat?" he asked.

"My work."

"Your work," he said, "if you'll pardon an observation, is highly erotic." A rash of gooseflesh spilled over his bare chest and shoulders. Although the room wasn't especially chilly, his lean, close-knit torso shivered. In contrast to his sun-freckled face, the skin under his clothing was pale, hairless, and smooth. "Such art has a rich tradition. Do you consider yourself part of it?"

"If I'm part of any tradition, it's a return to classical figurative painting."

Tahar stepped out of his corduroy trousers. The shivering had spread to his voice. "I notice all your models are aroused. Are you?"

"For me, it's strictly professional."

He pulled down his underpants. "I find it hard to believe you feel nothing when your models feel so much."

"I didn't say I feel nothing." Her lips crimped into a tight little smile. "But I channel my emotions."

There was no pretense that she wasn't staring at the appalling damage between his legs. Then she lowered her gaze to his feet, all of whose toenails had been extracted. Her angular, asymmetrical face was difficult for him to read. But it didn't bother Tahar that she remained silent. What mattered was that she didn't turn away, repulsed.

"Don't you agree," he said, "that art involves a sort of striptease for both the painter and the model?"

"You're getting way beyond my pay grade, Professor."

"I doubt that. I doubt there's any aspect of painting that you haven't considered. Or any aspect of the human anatomy."

"I'm with Francis Bacon. It's pointless to discuss art. If you can talk about it, why paint it?"

She suggested that he lie on the bed and motioned with her hand that he should make himself hard. There was a kind of discipline to her scene setting. She was a stickler for stage directions, determined to arrange things to appear spontaneous.

Tahar had his own agenda. He preferred her to bear witness to what had been done to him, challenging her to transform his mutilation into something not necessarily beautiful but bearable to her and to him.

"A man needs a little encouragement," he whispered. "Why don't you undress?"

"That's not part of the deal. You pose. I paint." From the night-table drawer, she fetched a pornographic magazine. "Maybe this'll help."

Saturated with color, couples performed sex acts in positions that defied logic and the laws of gravity. Their effect on Tahar was no more stimulating than the stick figures that had festooned the walls of his cell. He tossed the magazine aside and focused on Simone's painting of a florid, floral vulva.

She started a pen-and-ink drawing in a sketch pad. The room filled with the sound of fingernails on slate. "Keep touching yourself," she said.

"I'd rather you touch me."

"That's not going to happen. That's not what we're here for."

"We're here strictly for aesthetic purposes," he mocked her. "Have your lovers ever posed for you?" As his penis stiffened, its curve grew more pronounced, bending back on itself.

"Sure, some guys are show-offs." Her eyes flicked from him to the page.

A sharp ache forked up Tahar's thighs to his crotch. It reminded him of the trauma of the telephone. After his release from prison, the doctors he consulted had all been compassionate. But their questions had been impossible to answer. How would he rate his pain on a scale of one to ten? they asked. Numbers meant nothing; language was a waste of time. The shrieking claustrophobia of his confinement, the agony of his experience were inscribed indelibly on his flesh. Yet words could never capture any of it.

Was he capable of erections? The doctors had wanted to know. Was the pain worse when his penis was erect? Then they asked a question that Simone eventually got around to: "Can you have sex?"

"Is that an invitation? Or idle curiosity?"

"Aren't you the comedian."

"Seriously, why do you want to know?"

"Okay. It's none of my business."

"The sad truth is I haven't had a chance to try. Even prostitutes take one look, figure I have a disease, and send me packing. They lack your admirable sangfroid."

"That's me. Cold-blooded as a basilisk."

"That's not what I meant. I'm praising you for not recoiling. Would you like to hear how this happened?"

"Pablo told me you were tortured."

"That's the short version. 'God is in the details,'" he repeated his favorite adage. Then he described being beaten with a bicycle chain, waterboarded over and over, subjected to electric shocks, deprived for days of sleep, food, and sensory stimulus. "All in an effort to persuade me to talk. Even after they realized I didn't have any information of use to them, they kept torturing me."

Yet then, as now, he couldn't quit talking. It was his only release. Perhaps painting served that purpose for Simone—permitting her to lose track, if only temporarily, of some excruciating torment. He suspected that she had endured her own deep wounds. But she disclosed nothing about herself—just flipped the pages of her pad and continued sketching.

He discussed Algerian politics, linking public outrages to his personal afflictions. He paraphrased the novel he was reading, *The Secret Agent*, where Joseph Conrad contended that huge international revolutions started with private grievances disguised as creeds. He digressed and doubled back, attempting to reach her, to touch the right chord. He spoke of the past in the present tense and referred to Tlemcen as if it were next door, not on the far side of the Mediterranean. He recounted random anecdotes about North Africa, the pre-Islamic era, the Roman settlements in Algeria. "We were at the crossroads of the ancient world. Itinerant traders negotiated in a Babel of languages and hired translators who had parrots tattooed on their chests to advertise their services."

Snapping the sketch pad shut, Simone playfully jabbed her pen at him. "I should tattoo a parrot on your chest. You can get dressed now."

Embarrassed by her brusque dismissal, he disappeared into the bathroom and ran cold water over his wrists. Slowly his penis softened so that he could pull up his underpants. The face in the mirror belonged to a man he didn't recognize—a small nut-brown simian with baffled eyes. He longed to hide here amid Simone's sweet-smelling soaps and lotions, but she called out, "Are you okay?"

"I'm fine." Fully dressed, he strode into the studio. "Let's do this again."

"Sure. Whenever you need a break from your writing."

• • •

In fact, he had written little or nothing. He didn't need a break from work. He needed a breakthrough. He read *The Secret Agent* and hoped it might provide a template for his novel. He underlined a passage that resonated for him: "What is one to say of an act of destructive ferocity so absurd as to be incomprehensible, inexplicable, almost unthinkable, in fact, mad?" He marveled at Conrad's vast rogue's gallery of characters, ranging from the top to the bottom rungs of London society—corrupt politicians, cruel, self-righteous cops, idealistic revolutionaries, vicious agents provocateurs, nihilistic terrorists and antiterrorists whose tactics were two sides of the same coin. They committed atrocities to encourage their allies. They committed atrocities and blamed their opponents. Yet, try as he might, Tahar couldn't manage to steal the story and transpose it to North Africa.

Instead, he obsessed about Simone, killing hours until enough time had passed that he felt free to knock at her door again. Each time he did, she welcomed him a little less warmly than she had at first. "Shouldn't you be writing?" she said.

"I find posing for you is excellent preparation for my book. Our conversations may sound haphazard to you, but I'm testing narrative possibilities."

She gestured for him to undress. He did as instructed and never stopped talking. "In Arabic culture, traditional literature is the preserve of the upper classes. Plot and character are sublimated to surface brilliance. But great storytelling of the type that interests me, and I hope you, appeals to common people as well as intellectuals. It deals with life-and-death predicaments."

"Scheherazade," Simone suggested.

Yes, Tahar pictured himself playing that storytelling role with Simone—no different than he did with Spann. In both cases, his fate depended on carefully crafted narratives.

Simone switched from pen and ink to watercolors, and the background acoustics changed from dry scratching to the moist sibilance of a brush. She never showed him how she depicted him, and he didn't betray any desire to see it. He was well aware of how he looked—nothing at all like the men pinned to Simone's wall, perfectly shaped, bursting with unblemished health. "Have you heard of the Fregoli delusion?" he continued his talking cure.

"The what?" Her brush halted in midair, dribbling paint.

"It's a psychiatric disorder that leaves patients with the delusion that different people are all the same person. It's a rare condition."

"I should hope so."

"As an artist, I'm sure you can't conceive of any two faces looking interchangeable. But the men in your paintings—"

Simone let out a peal of laughter, bright as a party favor. "I get what you're driving at. Don't all cocks look the same? Well, no, they definitely don't."

"That wasn't what I meant," he lied. "I was going to ask how you view the place of your work in contemporary art."

"Really, Tahar, I have a hard time picturing my place in my own apartment building."

"Where is your apartment?'

"Tribeca."

"Is that a good area to live in?"

"Yeah, if you can afford it."

"Maybe Spann'll send me to New York. Where would you suggest I live?"

"There are plenty of places. Probably the State Department will make that decision."

"I'd prefer Manhattan because of its universities and its hospital facilities."

Simone shoved a stray hair off her face, inadvertently striping her cheek purple.

"Online," he said, "I've read about a medical procedure for my condition. The best surgeons are in New York."

She murmured something under her breath.

"In Algeria—anywhere in the Arab world—we couldn't have this conversation," he said. "Men and women never discuss sex."

"I thought we were discussing where you'd live."

Ignoring the barb, he plowed ahead. "For a brief period after Liberation, relations in Algeria between men and women improved, but then the Islamists undermined any chance for a secular society. Have you read Edward Said's *Orientalism*?"

"Paul recommended it. I'll get around to it one of these days."

"Said pointed out the paradox of foreign artists and authors portraying the Muslim world as primitive and repressive while at the same time treating it as a playground for their perverse fantasies. The French, for example, regarded sex as a local resource, no different from oil and agriculture."

"Stay still. Stop squirming."

"I wasn't aware I was squirming."

"Well, you are."

"The subject animates me. I may explore it in my novel—the sexual exploitation of the indigenous population. Take a great writer like Flaubert. The French government gave him a grant to travel to Egypt and catalog antiquities. In his leisure time—which seemed to be most of the time—he visited brothels and noted in a secret diary his fascination with the local custom of shaving pubic hair. He described 'naked cunts that looked as hard as bronze.'"

"That doesn't sound very attractive."

"Some men would disagree."

"Yes, some men always disagree."

"In North Africa, attitudes haven't changed much since Flaubert's day. There's constant tension between the sexes. I met an American woman in Tlemcen who was employed by an NGO to teach students how to become business entrepreneurs. She barely spoke French and didn't speak a word of Arabic. They assigned her a translator, a man—"

"Who had a parrot tattooed on his chest."

"Excuse me?"

"A bad joke. Forget it."

"They became friends, and he confided that he still lived with his parents. He couldn't afford to rent an apartment and marry. He confessed that he was a virgin and feared he would die one."

"I see where this is headed."

"No. He wasn't after sex with her. It mattered more to him to have a friend who empathized with his dilemma. He told her he loved a girl in his hometown, but they couldn't communicate because he didn't own a cell phone or a computer. So the American woman loaned him her smart phone."

"And he hacked into her bank account and stole all her money."

"No, this was sadder. He found snapshots of her and her family on her phone, and he showed them around, bragging that he had many American friends. The woman felt violated. She accused him of cyberstalking, and the director of the NGO fired the poor fellow."

Simone quit painting and began cleaning her brushes. Tahar added, "I may include this incident in my book. It shows how sexual misunderstanding can lead to problems, even violence. It can create a terrorist. There are seven steps to radicalization. Would you like to hear the list?"

"Please, Tahar, please." She plunked her brushes down. "I can't paint and listen to you at the same time. You've got to decide—are you here to pose or to talk?"

"Okay, I'll shut up."

"Don't be hurt; don't sulk. But let's call it a day."

CHAPTER XIII

The next morning, Simone and Tahar lingered at the breakfast table, alone except for Patsy, who sullenly slapped down bread, butter, jam, and coffee. Above the stove, pots and pans hung like a collection of polished clocks without hands or numbers.

"I'm burned out," Simone said. "I need a break from painting."

Tahar frowned at the news. "What will you do instead?"

"Maybe drive into the countryside. It's been months since I've been out of the city."

"I can't even leave the *carmen*, and now I need a haircut." Tahar combed his fingers through the frizziness above his broad, flat forehead.

"Let Patsy do it."

Hearing her name, Patsy glanced up, expectant, hostile.

"What about you?" he asked Simone.

"I'm afraid hairstyling isn't on my CV."

"You might enjoy developing a new specialty."

"No, thanks." She shoved back from the table

• • •

Simone traipsed upstairs to the tower, her shoes resounding on the scalloped steps. She wore a multicolored wool poncho that a gregarious shopkeeper in Little Morocco had bilked her into buying. He led her to believe it had been hand-loomed in the High Atlas by Berber women. Later she noticed a tag: the poncho had been mass-produced with synthetic fibers in Bolivia.

She recounted this to Paul and got a laugh from him. His room reminded her of a grad student's garret, strewn with clothes and books. It was messy, she decided, not dirty. Windows provided telescopic views in all directions and prevented the place from feeling cramped.

"Busy?" she asked.

"Not really. A few emails. Why aren't you in your studio?"

"I'm playing hooky. Why don't we take a drive?"

"No car."

"I'll rent one." Then she added, "We really need to talk."

He fetched the leather jacket she had bought him for Christmas. Again she remarked how much he looked like a metrosexual hipster. As they walked arm in arm down the dwindling streets of the Albaicín, he waited for her to get to the subject. But she stayed silent until they were in the Hertz office. There Simone produced an Amex platinum card and spoke brisk English to the agent. All business, she never called on Paul's Spanish when there was confusion over the collision damage waiver. The agent raised an eyebrow at Paul. But perhaps he was only puzzled that Simone wore Ray-Ban sunglasses indoors on an overcast day.

They headed east, with Simone at the wheel, whizzing

past stark, ugly housing tracts—*urbanizaciones*, billboards proclaimed. They looked like they had been built yesterday and might fall apart tomorrow. Big-box stores—Hypermarket and Brico Dépôt—hulked at the corners of a parking lot lined end to end with cars.

"We might as well be in New Jersey," she said.

"'Sweetest nut hath sourest rind,'" he replied.

"Burma-Shave."

"No, Shakespeare."

"For a guy who doesn't write, you're awfully literary."

"Yes, awfully. The benefit of running an arts residency."

Where the sprawling commercial area ended, they entered the vast agricultural expanse of the *vega*. Fields, freshly turned and fallow for the winter, alternated with stands of poplar trees, as precise as a military formation on parade. This late in the season, a last few golden leaves swam in the wake of the car.

"Those trees can't possibly have sprung up like that," Simone said.

"No, they were planted during Franco's regime. When I was a boy, you still saw signs praising him for supplying the people with *más agua, más árboles*. More water, more trees."

"So he wasn't all bad?"

"Depends who you talk to. My mother made him sound like the second coming of Satan. Worse than my father."

"It's all so long ago. Time to get over it," Simone said.

"Yeah, like the American South ever got over the Civil War. Franco went on executing his enemies into the late '40s."

"I didn't realize that."

"Still, he has his defenders. When the mailman delivers letters to the *carmen*, he always checks the postmarks. 'Ten days from America to Spain,' he'll hiss. 'Under Franco, it was five days.'"

Simone coaxed the cube-shaped SEAT up to 140 kph. "I know this makes me sound like the worst kind of person, but I love speed."

"No, the worst kind of person is someone like Franco, who ordered medical experiments on prisoners to discover if there was a physical cause of communism."

"We're not going to spend the day talking about Spanish politics, are we?"

"Not if you don't want to."

"I don't. Part of the reason I left the States was to escape the constant yammering about Trump."

"Tahar's surprised by your politics. He doesn't understand why you don't seem to have any. He admires artists who are *engagé*."

"Don't get me started on Tahar."

The poplar trees petered out, supplanted by vineyards that had been pruned into gnarled, knee-high twigs trussed together by twine. Farther on, solar panels spread over fields, acres and acres of rectangular installations that reflected gray clouds. Ancient stone walls didn't separate these plots so much as mold them together into a collage. Road signs supplied Arabic translations of Spanish towns in Kufic script.

"I trust you know where we're going," Simone said.

"Straight ahead and we'll hit the desert near Murcia. They shoot spaghetti Westerns there. Like to visit a film set?"

"I'm not in the mood. I just want to drive."

"I thought you wanted to talk."

"That too."

In the Guadix Basin, a zone that eons ago had been under water, there reared up what looked like coral reefs and submarine escarpments. In summer, they were dry as chalk. Now winter rains had rinsed off the dust and revealed vivid colors.

"I love this red-rock country," Paul said.

"Ocher," Simone corrected him.

"Okay, ocher."

Paul filled the dead air between them, marking time until Simone, usually so direct, decided to come around to whatever she had on her mind. Not that he was eager to hear it. He suspected she was anxious to clarify things between them. But then she puzzled him, saying, "I need to tell you about Tahar."

"Tahar?" It didn't seem possible that Patsy had been right and Simone was sleeping with the professor. "Let's pull over."

"I'd rather drive. The worst thing I ever did was invite him to pose for me. The second-worst thing was not calling it quits once I wised up. Now I don't have a clue how to get rid of him."

"How do you usually get rid of models?"

"I switch off Chat Random and they vanish. It's totally impersonal."

"And with Tahar, it's totally personal?"

"It's worse than personal. He's in my face, smothering me every second, sharing intimacies I didn't ask for."

"Let me take a wild guess. He wants to have sex with you."

"That's the least of it. Lots of models try to sexualize what we're doing. Even gay models claim I turn them on—when they're actually turning themselves on."

"Is that what Tahar does—turn himself on?"

"You've seen my work. It's what male models do when they pose for me."

"And female models?"

"That's different. I don't like their hands covering what I'm painting."

She swung down a narrow lane on the outskirts of Guadix and coasted through a neighborhood of cave dwellings carved into cliff faces. The facades of houses, thickly layered with white lime, had boxed geraniums on the window ledges and garlic bulbs braided around the doors. Signs in French and German welcomed paying guests.

"Shall we rent a room?" Paul asked. "A linguist from the *carmen* was researching the last speakers of Caló, a dying Spanish dialect. He spent weeks here."

"The whole place looks like it's dying."

"It's different in spring."

"Isn't everything?"

She drove on through empty streets where café and restaurant chairs were stacked and chained to tables. The road ended at a racetrack. A sign indicated that Circuito de Guadix was a test ground for Pirelli tires. Formula 1 cars sizzled around a course of hairpin curves.

Crunching over dry needles and cones, Simone parked in a copse of pines with discarded newspaper pages fluttering like dying swans on their limbs. When she removed her sunglasses, her eyes were red-rimmed, as if she had been crying and might start again.

"Tahar never stops talking," she said. "He tells me everything."

Paul chuckled. "I thought women liked a man who confided in them."

"Goddamnit, it's not funny." She curled sideways on the seat, her knees aimed at him. "How much do you know about Tahar?"

"No more than you. Some Islamic group kidnapped him. There's a fatwa against him, and he's appealing for asylum in the States."

"What's the holdup? Why's he still in Spain?"

"Spann explains that they're checking out his story. They're paranoid about terrorists pretending to be refugees, then setting up sleeper cells in the States."

"That's ridiculous. All they'd have to do is see Tahar naked to know he's telling the truth."

She blotted tears on her poncho. In the background, there was the nerve-wracking noise from the track. "Most of my models are happy to strip and masturbate," Simone said. "But Tahar's in it for other reasons. He wants me to realize how badly he was hurt. Because of what they did to him, he's got a condition, I forget the name. His cock is deformed, and when it gets hard, it bends back, and it's obvious he's in pain."

"But you go on painting him?"

"What else can I do?

"Stop."

"That's not what Tahar wants. He wants me to look at him; he wants me to listen to his stories. The last thing he wants is for me to stop. It's not enough that I pay attention and paint him. He wants to get into my head and convince me we have a special connection. This morning, he asked me to cut his hair."

"The poor guy. Poor you." He reached over and held her hand

She shrugged him off and grabbed an iPhone from her purse. "Now he's sending me snapshots." She held the screen in front of Paul's face and scrolled through gruesome close-ups of a vagina stitched shut.

"Are you sure Tahar sent these?" he asked. "I think I've seen them in art magazines."

"Yes. They're famous pictures of a performance artist named Kembra Pfahler who had herself sewn shut. Tahar means for me to equate what was done to him with female genital mutilation?"

Paul gently moved the iPhone away from his face. "I know you're angry and upset, but a little pity might go a long way with him."

"Pity's not all he's looking for. He's on my bed with his cock in his hand. But he's after me for more than sympathy or sex."

"Why not meet him out in the courtyard, away from your room, and explain how you feel?"

"How do you think I feel?" She crammed the phone back into her purse. "Tahar's stalking me. He wants to move to New York City so he can carry on modeling for me and I can be a receptacle for his sad story."

Out on the track, the cars shrieked at corners and screamed on the straightaways. As drivers downshifted, their engines backfired, loud as gunshots. Then they accelerated with the sound of ripped adhesive.

Paul lifted his eyes to the horizon of snowcapped mountains. It dumbfounded him that someone of Simone's sophistication and self-possession, an artist whose career was premised on female empowerment, could be unstrung by such a pathetic figure.

"Tahar's an academic," Paul said. "He'll listen to reason."

"Maybe from you he might. Not from me. I'm creeped out having him near me. He says there are surgeons in New York who specialize in his condition. He probably counts on me to be his nurse."

Paul couldn't suppress a smile.

"You still think it's funny?" Simone exploded. "The other day, he told me about an American woman at an NGO in Algeria. She accused a local hire of harassment and had him fired. Tahar claimed that's the kind of thing that turns men into terrorists. I think he's threatening me."

"Tahar's eager to escape terrorists, not become one."

"You're not around him. I am, and he scares me."

Paul spoke slowly and lowered his voice to calm her. "Okay, I'll talk to him."

"And tell him what?"

"I'll say you're finished painting him. You're going on to your next project, and he needs to back off."

"I could tell him that. I was counting on you to say his behavior is totally inappropriate. He's creating a hostile atmosphere and has to leave the *carmen*."

"For Chrissake, Simone, we're not on an American campus, operating under Title IX regulations. It's an arts residency for adults."

"And Tahar's acting like a child. A dangerous one."

It was on the tip of his tongue to say she was the childish one. "It's not my place to teach him American sexual etiquette."

"My God, you haven't understood a single word I've said."

"So say it again. What do you want me to do?"

"Get rid of him, just like you did Blessed."

"I explained before, Blessed was different. Tahar's a guest, a paying resident."

"If it's a matter of money, tell me how much it'll cost you to kick him out."

"Hey, hey, cool down. I can't just kick him out. He's here under US government protection."

"Protection from what?"

"From the fatwa against him. Uncle Sam's paying his expenses. Ten thousand bucks a month. They insisted I kick everybody else out. I argued it was no deal unless you stayed."

"I guess I should be grateful for small favors."

Her attitude, her sense of entitlement, rankled him, but he was reluctant to give in to his anger. "I'm the one who's grateful to have you here. You don't know what it's meant to me." He shied away from the specifics of his attachment—her smell, the texture of her skin, her shamelessness in bed. He loved everything Simone was that he feared he wasn't. "I'll make it clear to Tahar to leave you alone."

"I counted on more from you."

Rather than blurt something terminally cruel, he settled, as he often did, for a wisecrack. "Patsy tells me that every day."

"Maybe you should listen to Patsy."

"Maybe you should stop trying to act so tough."

"Maybe it's time for you to toughen up."

"Fuck this. I'm ready to go."

"What if I'm not ready?"

"Stay as long as you like. I'll hitchhike." He shouldered open the door. Immediately she gunned the SEAT to life, and his door slammed shut, throwing him back into the car as she circled around and sped toward Granada. Neither uttered a word until she flicked on the windshield wipers. "It's snowing," she said.

"It's sleet," he said.

CHAPTER XIV

Having eaten nothing after their argument, Paul was ravenously hungry the next morning, and although he hadn't drunk a drop of alcohol, he felt queasily hungover. Simone and he had made up, but he felt a tumbling sense of dread. He delayed going downstairs for breakfast, hoping to avoid Simone and Tahar until he decided what to do and how to do it.

When he couldn't put it off any longer, he went down and found Patsy washing dishes and Tahar at the table, sipping coffee from a bowl. The Algerian's hair looked as if it had been hacked short by a butcher knife. In spots, his bare, freckled scalp showed through. Other spots sprouted a few feathery hairs, like a hatchling fresh out of the shell. Still, Tahar smiled and chirped, "*Bonjour.*"

Above one ear, a puncture wound bled a thin drizzle. Tahar was dabbing it with a paper napkin.

"What the hell?" Paul exclaimed.

"*Alhamdulillah*, I'll survive," Tahar said.

"He asked me to cut his hair. I warned him to sit still." Patsy spoke in Spanish, her arms deep in soapsuds. "He wouldn't quit running his mouth."

Paul suspected that Patsy, in a fit of peevishness, had stabbed Tahar. Or had Tahar done something sexual to provoke her? He fetched the first-aid kit and doused a gauze pad with hydrogen peroxide. As he cleaned, then bandaged the cut, Tahar bared his neck like a condemned man resigned to the guillotine. "Do I need stitches?" he asked.

"I don't think so," Paul said.

"Don't blame me," Patsy said. "He wouldn't quit fidgeting."

On the floor around Tahar's chair lay the scattered hair Patsy had cut off. "Sweep this up." Paul said.

"He needs to collect the hair himself. Otherwise a witch could use it to cast a spell."

"I can't deal with this mumbo-jumbo. You two sort it out. I've got errands to run."

"I'll hold on to the peroxide bottle," Tahar said. "I may need more."

Paul hesitated outside the *carmen.* The Hand of Fatima door knocker hung behind his head. For a moment, he couldn't decide which way to turn. Then ancient muscle memory guided him down an alley he had followed as a kid when his mother had sent him out to buy bread.

Too narrow for cars, too bumpy for motorbikes, the alley, his mother had believed, was safe for her seven-year-old son. But Paul had viewed it then as a perilous labyrinth, a Dungeons and Dragons challenge that alternately thrilled and terrified him. Sprinting down the path, he feared a fanged monster would lunge from Convento Santa Isabel de Real and devour him. Today, as he trudged along the alley, he felt once again that he might be swallowed up, a victim of his own bad choices.

The café tables in the Plaza San Miguel Bajo were vacant, their umbrellas reefed like sails in stormy weather. He sat outside Mesón El Yunque, where a waiter in a fleece-lined vest served him strong *café con leche* and a *ración* of churros. For Paul, this was the equivalent of the *petite madeleine*, drenching him in memories and rumination.

• • •

The previous night, on the drive back from Guadix, fearing that he and Simone were finished, he had decided to let the affair die a quick death. Better that than fumble around, attempting artificial respiration. There was nothing to discuss except when and under what circumstances she left the *carmen*.

Still, he seethed inside. What the hell had been on his mind when he'd allowed himself to become embroiled with this woman? Sure, they fit. The Gypsy's curse. But every time she didn't get her way, her stubborn sense of entitlement, her grandiosity, kicked in. How had he deluded himself that Simone could be the fixed point in his life, a stay against the world he felt crumbling around him?

The drive through sleet to the *carmen* passed in silence. Simone went straight to her room, while Paul retreated to the tower and calculated as dispassionately as possible what the breakup would cost him. He avoided the emotional part and concentrated on the practical consequences. He had hoped that Simone would attract other high-profile artists. If she stalked off angry and hell-bent on revenge, he could forget that. On the other hand, if he did as she demanded and evicted Tahar, what would happen to the Algerian? What sort of payback might Spann exact?

Caught up by the quarrel in his head, he kept fretting until he heard a muffled knock at his door. Simone was teetering on the top step in bare feet. Wet from the shower, her hair dripped onto the indigo burnoose she wore as a nightgown, plastering it in spots to her skin. She didn't wait for him to speak. She covered his mouth with hers, backing him over to the bed, and tumbled on top of him.

This was the sort of apology he should have expected from Simone. She never actually said she was sorry. It was, he suspected, a down payment on the next demand she'd make. Not that this stopped him, not that it dissuaded him for an instant.

Afterward, they lay crowded together on the single bed, their legs entwined. Then she raised herself on an elbow. "There's something I need to tell you."

He imagined she might announce that she loved him. With a sharp clench of his heart, he thought she might say she was pregnant.

"Getting back to that question of the worst thing I ever did—" She untangled her legs from his. "I knew your father. This was in Florida when I was a grad student. He taught one of my courses." After a pause, she added, "I slept with him."

His immediate reaction was that this couldn't conceivably be true. She was proving how much pain she could cause.

"This was years ago," she said. "It didn't last long. Not that it didn't matter to me at the time."

Paul sat up so abruptly that he almost knocked them out of

bed. He caught her and saved them both from falling. She mistook this for a loving embrace and clung to him.

"Why are you telling me this?" he asked.

"I thought you should know."

"Why now? Tonight?"

"Should I have told you the day I got to Granada? Or mentioned it in my application for a residency?" Although she was shaking in his arms, her voice was firm.

With the clarity of a thunderclap, he saw now why she had asked so many questions about his father. Peter Stewart was the lover who had brought her water in his mouth. The Lorca scholar. The controlling man who had argued that she hadn't actually witnessed the green flash. The one who had kept his eyes open during sex, making her feel like a watched pot. Paul believed he understood everything but again asked, "Why?"

"I was looking for a quiet place to work. Peter had told me about the *carmen* and about you."

"I can imagine what he said."

"No, Pablo, I don't think you can."

"Don't call me Pablo."

"It's the name he used. He spoke of you with a lot of tenderness. Almost wistfulness. Naturally I was curious to meet you. That's the best explanation I can offer."

He understood this was her "best explanation." He didn't have it in him to probe for the worst.

"Lie down." She soothed him with her words and her hands, which moved over him with the care of an art restorer assessing a damaged canvas. "I'd like you to hear how it ended between us."

"I don't want to know."

"It might help you understand him and maybe yourself."

The tale Simone insisted on telling him started in the shape of a campus novel. A female graduate student, recently divorced, encounters an older professor with a reputation that attracts almost as many women as it repels. Those who are tempted to sleep with him constitute a self-selecting cohort. Simone was savvy enough to know this, but it didn't discourage her.

Still plausibly handsome in late middle age, Peter Stewart wore his wrinkles and scars like a mask, she said. A cynic's disguise. But every once in a while, a child's face broke through. "He didn't need to seduce women," Simone went on. "They seduced themselves. There was all the tantalizing gossip about his connection to US intelligence. He showed his guns in his bureau to every woman he brought into his bedroom. He played it cool, borderline insulting with me. When I told him I painted, he said, 'Artists are like horseshit. You spread them over a wide field, and they make flowers grow. Pile them up in one spot, and they just stink. You should get away from these academic assholes and take a trip with me to the Caribbean.'"

Her account of that trip mirrored Paul's own memories. The seaplane flight to a spit of land in a blue immensity. The jarring ride in a Land Rover across a mountain range to a cove where the sand sparkled like glass splinters. Green foam, like a lime daiquiri, at the edge of the shore. A shack of pine boards and palm fronds. The inflatable dinghy, the daily spearfishing, the Luger strapped to his hip.

Paul was at the point of objecting that she was plagiarizing him when she threw in details that he remembered but hadn't mentioned to her. On the dock where the pilot tethered the seaplane, there had been a bright red British telephone booth, defunct for decades, strangled inside and out by tropical vines. In the jungle, near the salt pond behind the beach, an abandoned Lincoln Continental convertible was sunk to its axles in mud.

"Your father could be a bit overwhelming," Simone said.

"More than a bit."

"He was an exciting man to be around, but scary, like a car spinning out of control. Women should have run away from him. Instead, they threw themselves under the wheels. When he told me we were going shark fishing, I told him I had zero interest in getting in a boat with a guy carrying a gun."

"'But you went," Paul said.

"Yes, I went. He wasn't a man who understood the word 'no.' And it obviously meant a lot to him to have me along."

For their excursion to the Francis Drake Channel, the rubber dinghy wouldn't do, she said. Peter borrowed a native-built dory—flat-bottomed, high-sided, pushed along by an antiquated outboard engine. Beyond the cove, the sea darkened to a shade of bottle green that broke into long, white rollers. Although the dory felt indestructible, it didn't feel unsinkable, and Simone said she grabbed the gunwales on either side.

"'Afraid a shark'll jump in and gobble you up?' Peter teased me. When we started to take on water, he handed me a calabash and ordered me to bail. Like he was Captain Ahab. Then he cut the motor, and we drifted through a field of Clorox bottles tied to fish traps. Your father grabbed a bottle and hauled up the line. The trap looked like a cage alive with exotic birds," Simone said. "He dumped a fish into the boat and baited it on a big rusty hook. Then he pushed the trap overboard and tossed in the hook. My job, he said, was to help him reel the shark in next to the boat so he could shoot it. He promised we'd have shark steaks for dinner. He unholstered the gun and held it on his lap. This struck me as stupid beyond words, but I was too afraid to say anything."

Simone, still in Paul's arms, still caressing him with rough hands, described bumping from plastic bottle to bottle, the current carrying them along at a fast clip, the cool morning air burning off and midday sun beating down. The heat, the pitching and yawing made her seasick.

"I tried to be a good sport," she said. "When we floated toward a hotel on Saint John's, I joked that we should dock there for lunch. He just started the engine and steered us back to the Clorox bottles. I stopped bailing; water sloshed over my feet. 'Let's go back before we sink.'"

"'This barge'll never sink,' Peter said in a fake old-salt brogue.

"'I appreciate this is a treat for me,' I told him. 'But you needn't bother.'

"'No bother.'

"It was then that I began to wonder whether we were out here to fish for sharks or something else. He never rebaited the hook. He didn't watch the line. He let me hold it while he panned his eyes over the ocean, searching for something."

"Like what?" Paul asked.

"Like maybe he was on a mission and expected to meet someone."

"That doesn't make sense. If he was on a mission, why would he bring you along?"

"To be a witness."

"A witness to what?"

"A witness to his intelligence career. To impress me and prove everything that I'd heard was true. But nobody showed up, and he got more frustrated and furious. By then I was furious too. A swarm of seagulls and pelicans swooped over us. 'They're vultures waiting to pick our bones when we die,' I said."

"'You think so? I'll take care of that.' Calm as you like, Peter aimed the Luger and fired off a clip. Pelicans and seagulls spiraled into the ocean like they were diving for fish."

"'Ever see such goddamn great marksmanship?' Peter gloated. 'It's hard to hit a clay pigeon with a shotgun. But seabirds at this range with a handgun, that's Olympic-level shooting.'

"It hit me then that I wasn't with some fascinating older man, a mentor who had a lot to teach me. I was out in a boat in the middle of the ocean with an armed, deranged person. After we flew back to Florida, I broke off all contact with him. I dropped out of grad school and left town. I was afraid he'd kill me."

"I doubt that," Paul said. "His greatest threat was always to himself. He used to quote a line from William Carlos Williams: 'The perfect man of action is the suicide.'"

"You were never afraid of him?"

"I was always afraid of him."

"They say suicide runs in families."

"Don't worry about me. I'm not self-destructive." To Paul's ears, this rang like false bravado. Simone didn't say how it sounded to her.

A moment later, she told him, "Peter may have been a lousy

mentor, but one of his lessons stuck with me. He showed me how much a man can get away with. I decided as a woman to allow myself the same privilege of pushing the limits."

They remained awake, silent now, in the cold, wind-buffeted tower. A perplexing sense that he had traveled full circle stole over Paul. Having vowed for so long that he wouldn't become his father, here he was in bed with another of Peter Stewart's lovers. He couldn't fathom why Simone had delayed so long in telling him the truth. Would it have stopped their affair from ever starting? Or made it inevitable? Did she view her past as an indissoluble bond between them? Or as an excuse for why Paul and she couldn't stay together?

• • •

These questions and others persisted the next day at the café table outside Mesón El Yunque. The caffeine and the sugar high from the churros should have crystallized his thoughts. Instead, they skittered off in all directions. He pictured Blessed, freezing on the streets. Which brought to mind Tahar. If Paul kicked him out, how would Tahar survive?

As if conjured up by Paul's unquiet mind, Bill Spann bobbed across the plaza in his quilted ski jacket like a cartoon figure fashioned out of helium-filled balloons.

"What the hell are you doing out here in the cold?" Spann shouted.

"I was wondering the same about you."

"Patsy suggested where to look for you."

"A lucky guess on her part."

Spann dragged a wrought-iron chair up to the table, its legs twanging on the cobblestones. Sunburned skin had peeled from his nose. On his wrist, where a watch was missing, a white stripe separated his pink hand from his pink arm. He drew deeply on a cigarette.

"Did you ever find out anything about my father?" Paul asked. "Whether he was actually a US intelligence agent?"

"I made a couple preliminary inquiries. No feedback yet. I've been busy in Algeria. Ever been there?"

Paul shook his head.

"Fascinating country, in its turd-world way. I liaised with some local antiterrorist teams. They have a lot to teach us about our raghead friends."

"Things Tahar hasn't already filled you in on?"

"Filling things in isn't his strong suit. How much of his manuscript have you read?"

"Not a word. I don't pry into what residents are writing."

"I haven't read anything either. He keeps putting me off, promising I'll see it once it's polished."

"It takes years to finish a novel."

"Uncle Sam doesn't have that kind of time." Spann groped inside his parka and produced a thick envelope. "Before I forget, let's square our account. Close the books, so to say."

"Is Tahar leaving?"

"It won't be long now."

"Where's he going?" Paul tucked the envelope into his back pocket, hopeful that he might not have to evict Tahar after all. The State Department was about to do it for him.

"Normally that's classified. In this case, it's better to bring you up to speed so everything goes smooth at the end. We're debating whether to put him on a plane back to Algeria or rendition him to a place that specializes in enhanced interrogation. The second choice is expensive, and the desk jockeys at Langley are always worried about dollars."

"More than they worry about what'll happen to Tahar?"

"Don't get all sanctimonious. You have to understand the situation."

"What's changed? What about asylum for him in the States?"

Spann filched a churro from Paul's plate and crunched it between his front teeth. "Your *carmen* is . . . I'll call it a gray site. There's a school of thought that Tahar belongs in a black site."

Paul couldn't conceal his increasing agitation. "I thought you'd at least wait until he finished his novel. I thought—"

"Stop thinking. Tahar, it turns out, has been feeding us fiction from the get-go. His résumé, start to finish, is fake news. Algerian intelligence had no trouble proving Tahar's a bullshit artist."

"They can't claim he wasn't tortured," Paul said. "Look at the pictures Simone painted. He's got scars and burns all over his body."

"Quite a lady, that Simone." Spann's leer looked almost comical. "I agree Tahar's far from in tip-top shape. I bet he still gets nosebleeds from being waterboarded. But my job was to find out who did all that damage to him. The Algerians were happy to take the credit.

Spann expelled plumes of condensation along with cigarette smoke. The mixture fogged Paul's vision. Through the haze, he said, "I don't follow."

"Come on, Pablo, catch up. You're smarter than this."

"Why would Algerian intelligence torture him?"

"I'd just be wagging."

"Wagging?"

"Wild-ass guessing. The reason doesn't really matter. Maybe he just pissed them off." Spann was gnawing at another churro. "Students had reported him for antiregime comments. He was warned to knock it off and get with the program. But he kept publishing stuff in left-wing journals about politicians pocketing kickbacks from foreign oil companies. The government demanded to know where he got his information. They plugged him into an electric outlet, and he lit up like a neon bulb."

Spann brushed the sugar from his fingertips with the classic friction of a money changer. "You probably noticed, Tahar is quite the talker. With a little encouragement, he confessed that he didn't have any inside sources. He's a library guy. He read what journalists in Paris reported and spat it back out in Arabic."

"If he confessed, why did they torture him?"

"To squeeze out the last drop. To deliver a few extra jolts and teach him a lesson. Instead, Tahar, the dumb fuckwit, doubled down. Soon as he was out of prison, he applied to us for asylum, promising to supply firsthand info. The problem is the US already knows all about Algeria's torture program. We acted as advisers. Tahar's got nothing to trade."

"Jesus."

"Jesus, Allah, and Joseph." Spann laughed.

"Couldn't the Americans grant him a humanitarian visa?"

Spann shifted ponderously inside his parka. "Maybe if he had gone through regular channels and filed honest papers, who knows? Some sweetheart at the State Department might have rubber-stamped his application. But he lied after signing a sworn statement that he was telling the truth. And he didn't stop there. He piled bullshit on top of bullshit about a mullah issuing a fatwa against him."

"The fatwa's on the Internet. I've seen it," Paul said.

"So are ads for penis enlargement. You believe everything you read? We don't. There are guys at Fort Meade that can unscramble anything online. They found out he posted the fatwa against himself."

"The poor bastard. All he wanted was to move to America and get medical treatment."

"That's not all he wanted. He expected a university job and a publishing contract and CIA support to have his book translated and distributed internationally. Tahar knew the rules, and he didn't play by them. Now we need to decide whether he's a run-of-the-mill con man or an ISIS asset."

"Tahar's a nutty college professor. Nothing more."

"What are you willing to bet? Your life? Hundreds of lives? He could be a sleeper sent to the States like those 9-11 clowns. Couple years from now, he could climb out of his spider hole and blow up the White House."

"You're the one who ought to be writing fiction."

"Playing out scenarios is what I do."

"You're not playing at anything. You're setting him up to be tortured again. Maybe killed."

"I don't get my rocks off by renditioning people. There's always a chance he'll make a convincing case that he's clean."

"Then what'll happen to him?"

"We'll repatriate him to Algeria. They might decide Tahar's a pathetic dickhead and they don't need to fool with him anymore. Best case, he resettles in Tlemcen and pees sitting down the rest of his life."

Spann stood up and stamped his cold feet. "Now that we've had our little chat, naturally, softy that you are, you'll be tempted to give him a heads-up. My advice—no, my warning—keep your trap shut unless you'd like Homeland Security to pay you a visit."

"I'm a Spanish citizen. This is my homeland."

"We know you have two passports. That doesn't make a damn bit of difference. The US has excellent relations with the Spanish, who I predict would be happy to investigate your, what do you call it? arts colony and discover dozens of legal infractions."

"Anybody ever tell you you're a prick?"

"All the time. Sorry you personally feel that way. I've gotten a kick out of our conversations. It's a nice change of pace doing business with a gentleman and scholar, not another whacked-out Arab. I was hoping we could do this again. Maybe turn your place into a permanent site for debriefings."

"You're out of your fucking mind."

"Suit your sad-ass self. I intend to collect Tahar at the end of the week. I'm counting on a clean, quick transfer. No melodrama, no monkeyshines. I'll have backup. *Comprende*?"

"*Comprendo.*"

• • •

Unsteady in the wind, Spann crossed the cobblestones, in his puffy coat. Paul sat with the dregs of his coffee and churros and tried to convince himself that he wasn't to blame. Then, returning to the *carmen*, he walked by the convent that had been converted into a boutique hotel. The parking garage beneath Huerta de Carlos exhaled the stench of garbage and exhaust fumes. He ducked into Chefchaouen, a Moroccan restaurant painted pale blue to ward off the evil eye. Ordering a glass of Chaud Soleil wine, he drank it and bought a bowl of *harira* to take away. A pathetic offering for Tahar.

Since childhood, Paul had regarded the Albaicín as an island shut off from the surrounding city. Virtudes's account of its brave, suicidal holdout during the Civil War had heightened his sense of inhabiting a fortress. But now, carrying a plastic container of fast-cooling soup, he had no sense that he occupied a safe refuge. The walls had been breached; the enemy was within.

Outside Tahar's room, Paul listened to Spann's relentlessly mocking voice and to Tahar's reedy, pleading replies. What was the point of interrupting unless Paul had something more than soup to offer? He moved along the hall to Simone's room. She looked tired and drawn, the sun streaks in her hair faded.

"I thought you might be hungry." He handed her the soup, which she set aside without a glance.

"Have you talked to Tahar?" she asked.

"Not yet. His head was bleeding. Patsy's scissors slipped while she was cutting his hair. I had to bandage him."

"I doubt it was an accident. Patsy's such a witch."

"Then Spann showed up and needed to talk to me."

"A perfect chance to tell him that Tahar has got to go. But I bet you blew it."

He felt heat flare on his face. He was tempted to say something hurtful and final. Instead, he told her, "Tahar's leaving at the end of the week."

"Why didn't you say so?" She hugged him. "Thanks, sweetheart."

"I didn't have a thing to do with it. Spann made the decision. Or the people who run him did."

"You don't sound happy. Are they sending him to the States? Not to New York, I hope."

He flopped into an overstuffed chair with stubby legs that ended in griffin's claws. Simone perched on its arm, leaning against him.

"Wherever he winds up, it won't be New York," Paul said.

"Thank God."

As he gave her the gist, not the minutiae of what Spann had revealed, he had an impulse to defend Tahar. He feared she'd find him more odious than ever and view his scheming as every bit as repugnant as his behavior with her. "Spann says they'll probably send him back to Algeria—unless the State Department decides to rendition him to a black site."

"Oh, God, not Guantanamo! What went wrong?"

"There were holes in his story."

"The one he's writing?"

"The one he told Spann."

"Tahar had his hopes so high," Simone wailed. "This is going to crush him."

"Let's be nice to him in his last few days here."

CHAPTER XV

Tahar's skull hurt. Not just where Patsy had stabbed him but everywhere, inside and out. Thoughts spat from his brainpan like grease from a skillet. It had been the same in prison. He couldn't quit thinking, imagining an escape. If only he had had a pen and paper then, he believed he could have constructed a ladder of language.

Now, when he had at hand all the resources to write a book, he found it impossible to put a word on paper. Idly, he scrolled through terrorist websites. It flabbergasted him how much fetid material he found online. How could any government hope to stamp out terrorism if it couldn't staunch the flow of footage of blank-eyed bombers, men dictating farewell videos, veiled women sewing suicide vests, masked executioners beheading infidels?

The Internet struck him as a snake eating its tail. What was the word for that? Tahar typed in the question, and "ouroboros" flashed on the screen, trailed by definitions. The symbol had first appeared in Egyptian funerary texts, representing the cycle of death and rebirth. Currently computer geeks used it as a meme for the feedback loop.

Tahar skimmed a discussion of cultures that regarded the snake as an icon of evil, the source of original sin, a surrogate penis. The word "penis" linked him to Peyronie's disease, and the screen flooded with photos of men with cosmic-joke sexual organs wrenched into odd shapes. Close-ups of surgical procedures intended to deal with the disorder—penises cut open like sausages and straightened with plastic rods—made the cure looked crueler than the condition.

Why had Simone ever asked him to pose for her? How had he ever allowed himself to believe that she didn't find him disgusting? Her docile reaction to his disfigurement had deceived him into thinking that after his surgery in the States, they might stay together.

That was before she became as ill-tempered as Patsy, who this morning had knotted a dish towel around his neck like a hangman's noose and ordered him to hold still. Infuriated by his fidgeting, she shouted something in mangled English that he finally managed to understand: "Simone and Paul, they fucking."

Tahar jerked his head, and the scissors sliced open his scalp. Blood trickled down his neck and fell, along with frizzy locks of his hair, to the floor. He had trusted and confided in Simone more intimately than anyone else in his life, and she had betrayed him.

Later, when Spann showed up for their weekly session, Tahar protested that he was in no shape to talk. But the fat man frog-marched him out of the kitchen to his room. "What happened to your head?"

"Patsy cut my hair."

"Looks like she worked you over with hedge clippers." Spann snooped around Tahar's studio, snatching up the bottle of hydrogen peroxide, giving it a shake.

"Disinfectant for my cut," Tahar said.

Spann thumbed through papers on the desk, notes that Tahar had cribbed from the Internet. He read passages in French and demanded that Tahar translate those into Arabic.

"Do you think I'm sending and receiving secret messages?" Tahar asked.

"I'm not paid to think, just to be thorough. You sure the cook didn't stab you because you pinched her ass? She looks like your type," Spann said.

"I'd say she's more your type."

"My fucking days are far behind me. Diabetes. High blood pressure. Heart problems."

"You're still a young man."

"With a very old dick. Beat it while it's hot, that's what the blacksmith says. I wasted my best years lifting weights, eating steroids, playing football for sadistic coaches. Now I'd need six pounds of Viagra to jump-start me. How's the novel coming?"

"Slowly."

Spann leaned as far forward as his belly would permit. Behind him, the barred window presented a slotted view of dead plants in the garden. "What's the problemo?"

"Holed up here like a hostage, it's not easy to be creative. And you haven't been very reassuring."

"Funny thing. That's how I'd describe you—not very reassuring."

"I told you everything you asked. I've answered the same questions over and over."

Spann unzipped his parka, with a rasp releasing his immense paunch. "Look, Professor, I'm like a pistol. I shoot where I'm aimed. I ask what they want to know."

"And I've cooperated."

Spann was tamping a cigarette against his thumbnail. "I paid a little visit to Algeria, to your hometown. Do you miss it?"

"A few things," Tahar drawled to disguise the tremor in his voice. "Friends. Certain foods. Contact with students."

"Are you in touch with any friends or students?"

"No."

"None?"

"No one. You ordered me to cut off all contact."

"You don't Skype? You don't FaceTime or text?"

"Don't take my word for it. I'm sure you have ways of checking."

"Indeed we do." Spann sat spraddle-legged, manspreading, hogging maximum space. "Which is why we're curious about your fixation with terrorist websites."

"Research for the book." He tidied some loose pages Spann had just pawed through.

"That clears up everything except why you're obsessed with bomb-making."

"My book is about terrorists, and that's what they do. They make bombs."

"You're the expert, Professor. Tell me more."

"I never claimed to be an expert on terrorism. My expertise, my experience, is in being terrorized. I've already described that. Why am I still in Spain, not in the United States?"

Spann raised his hands in surrender. "I'm on your side. The trouble is some folks aren't 100 percent sure whose side you're on."

The sentence sank into him, as sharp as the blades of Patsy's scissors. Tahar decided it was best to say nothing.

"There are bureaucrats," Spann resumed, "who survive by covering their asses. Couple of agents decided your interview sounded like a rehash of what anyone could read online."

"Do they think I faked my torture?" His voice rose as he stood up and started to unbuckle his belt.

"Keep your pants on, Professor. Save that for Simone. Sources in Algeria confirm that you were tortured. The question is who did it to you and why."

Tahar felt he had been inching down a dark tunnel, fearing a trap at every step. Then a door yawned wide, and he found himself teetering at the brink of an abyss.

"Lemme remind you," Spann said, "when you applied for asylum, the fine print stressed that any falsehood is a federal offense."

Tahar had an urge to plunge over the edge, confess, and close his eyes to the hard ground racing up to smash him. Instead, he said quietly, "From the first day we met, I admitted I couldn't identify the men who kidnapped me. They didn't wear ID badges. They wore masks. How can I say whether it was ISIS or AQIM or some other group?"

Spann exclaimed, "Fido." He might have been calling a dog.

"You reach a fork in the road, and FIDO's the word—Fuck it. Drive on."

He pitched to his feet. "I'll be back at the end of the week. Be ready to mount up and move on."

"Move on where?"

"We don't discuss itineraries in advance. All the better to keep the bad guys guessing."

"It's cruel to keep me guessing too." Rising, Tahar suffered a rush of dizziness.

"You'll know soon enough."

"I need to know now. There are medical appointments I'd like to make. American universities to contact about jobs."

"That's exactly why we keep it secret. You go shooting off emails to the States, the other side'll track your every step. Just pack your bags and be ready."

When Spann left, Tahar felt that his life was racing him toward a conclusion he had no idea how to prepare for. He couldn't comprehend why Spann hadn't taken him away today. Then it hit him that he was a lab rat in a labyrinth. They were watching to see whether and where he would run. A real terrorist in this situation would have a plan B—an emergency contact in Spain, a cutout elsewhere in Europe. But Tahar had nothing.

He gazed at the brushed silver lid of his computer, at the perfect apple with a single bite mark. He felt . . . he couldn't say what he felt apart from fear and sadness. When there was a knock at the door, his instinct was not to answer. But then Simone called his name, and he opened up.

"Where have you been?" she said.

"Hiding. Patsy scalped me. I look too ridiculous to be seen in public."

"No, you don't. I'm about to paint—if you'd like to pose."

He followed her down the hallway, which smelled of floor polish and was slippery under his tasseled loafers. Her room was warmer than his. Because of her body heat, he supposed.

She didn't look her best. Washed clean of makeup, she had crow's-feet at the corners of her eyes and vertical lines on her upper lip. But her scent was one he would recognize anywhere—an intoxicating compound of perfumed soap and shampoo. He suffered a powerful urge to touch her and, almost as intense, an impulse to talk to her.

"I'll be in the bathroom," she said. "Why don't you undress?"

He removed his shoes and socks, then his trousers and underpants. On the night table lay a Dopp kit of miniature cosmetics—a courtesy gift for first-class airline passengers.

Behind the bathroom door, there was the sound of splashing water. Was it the bidet? In a flash fantasy, he imagined Simone emerging naked and sliding into bed beside him. He gripped his genitals.

Simone, fully clothed, came out and sorted through her brushes. Tahar continued stroking himself, telling her that his time at the *carmen* was about to end. He had to leave soon but didn't know where he was going.

"Paul mentioned something." She was mixing colors on her palette.

"Mentioned what?" he asked.

"Just that you might be leaving in a few days."

This puzzled him. Why had Spann stressed secrecy, then revealed this to Paul?

"It's a pity," he said, "that you and I didn't get a chance to tour Granada."

"I've seen enough to satisfy me," she said.

"I guess Paul showed you around."

"Yes, the high spots."

"Did he take you to Sospiro del Moro?"

"What's that?"

"A hill overlooking the city. Legend has it that Boabdil, the last ruler of Granada, paused there as he fled the conquering Christians. His mother was with him. Some historians claim that Christopher Columbus witnessed the scene. That's probably apocryphal."

"So many interesting stories," she mused.

"Life consists of stories we tell ourselves and ones we hear from other people. In prison, I clung to that consolation," he said, clinging now to his crooked penis. "As for Boabdil, the story is that he gazed back at the kingdom he had lost, sighed, and shed tears."

"Touching." Simone concentrated on the devastation between his thighs—the purple scorch marks, the scarred flesh.

"But his mother was a tough old bird. She told him, 'You cry now like a woman because you weren't man enough to save the last outpost of Islam in Spain.'"

"Stay still. Put your hand back where it was."

"Are you sure Paul didn't say where they're sending me?"

"He didn't tell me anything."

"You know where I'd like to go. But guess where the US government plans to send me?"

"No idea."

"Take a guess."

"I'm not good at guessing games." Her voice brimmed with annoyance, but her brushwork never faltered. She dabbed at the palette once, twice, three times.

"You can be sure they won't send me to the States."

She murmured that she was sorry.

"I'm guessing they'll pack me off to Algeria," he said, "where I'll probably be tortured again. Or else they'll rendition me for enhanced interrogation at a black site."

She reached for a rag, scrubbing her large, rough hands. "I hate hearing this. Why would they do that?"

Tahar saw no purpose in withholding the truth. "Because I lied about who tortured me. And I put false statements in my asylum application."

"Can't they overlook that?"

"I hoped they would. But Spann goes strictly by the book. Perhaps if I had help."

"What kind of help?" She stepped to the night table, took a vial of fingernail-polish remover out of the Dopp kit, and swabbed her fingers and palms.

"Take me to New York with you." He didn't infuse this with half the emotion he felt. Still, his plea froze her in place.

"I can't. Not if the US has already turned you down."

"We could fly to Canada. I'll apply for asylum there, then cross into the States. Sooner or later, I'll get a job and repay you."

"Canada won't let you in without a visa. Do you even have a passport?"

"Spann has it."

"I can't believe what a bastard he is. You have rights," Simone said. "Why not apply for asylum in Spain?"

It wearied him that she would ask such a question. It was as if Simone had never passed through Little Morocco, never noticed refugees begging in the streets, sleeping in doorways, digging for scraps of food in dumpsters. "How could I survive," he asked, "without papers, without money?"

"At least you'd be alive and not tortured."

Tahar sat upright in bed. "Spann wouldn't let me wander off. He'd have the Spanish arrest me."

"When I'm in New York," Simone said, "I'll sell the pictures I painted of you and wire some money."

"When would that be?"

"Whenever I'm finished here."

"You mean finished with Paul?"

"I mean finished with my project," she snapped.

"I have to have help by the end of the week. Not months from now. What would you do if Paul needed help?"

"Paul doesn't have anything to do with this."

"Of course he does. Spann pays him to hold me here."

"No one's holding you. This isn't a jail."

"For me, it's a jail. You can leave anytime. Or stay and keep sleeping with Paul."

"My private life is none of your damn business. It's time for you to go." But she was the one edging toward the door.

"You do nothing except exploit me."

"Oh, please! I didn't force you to pose for me."

"You didn't have to force me. You only had to ask. I was grateful that you looked at me and listened. You led me to believe I mattered."

"I didn't lead you on in any way. You knew the deal from the start."

"The things I told you, our talks about my plans and my time in prison, meant nothing to you."

"Stop it, Tahar." She kept inching away from him.

He sprang off the bed. "To you, I'm no different, no better than the strangers on Chat Random."

"This is sick."

"Yes, I'm sick. I'm mutilated. Still, you wanted me to model." He crowded closer.

"I promised to send you money. I can give you some now."

"I don't want money. I want you to touch me. I want to touch you." He shot out a hand and seized her arm. "You touch Paul. Why won't you touch me?"

"I'm going to scream." Her voice cracked; she was already screaming.

"Go ahead and holler. Maybe Paul will be a hero and rescue you." He twisted her hand down toward his penis, and at her touch, the pain he experienced was pitched at a level that exceeded his powers of endurance.

Simone yanked free and raced from the room. Tahar didn't chase her. Wave after wave of shame washed over him, drowning him in an abscess of self-loathing. He dressed and brought the bottle of fingernail-polish remover to his room, locking himself in and the rest of the world out.

For the first time in decades, he attempted to pray. The Koran had been pounded into him as a child like gold leaf hammered onto a pillar in the mosque. But the suras that swam to mind made him quake with foreboding. Tahar feared he would never be forgiven. He couldn't forgive himself. He couldn't forgive Simone. He had lost everything except a hatred and rage huge enough to consume the whole world.

CHAPTER XVI

A scream, loud and shrill, spiraled up the staircase. Paul assumed it was Patsy cursing in the kitchen at a saucepan that had boiled over. Then he recognized Simone's voice and rushed from the tower. She was at the bottom of the stairs, her hands clapped to her ears as if to deafen herself against her own hysteria.

He rushed to her, but she recoiled from his touch. "Do you know what he did to me?"

"Who?"

"Tahar." Her hands dropped from her ears. "I warned you he was crazy. I was painting him, and he grabbed me and made me touch his cock. I begged you to get rid of him. But you said be nice to him."

"I didn't say to go on painting him."

Simone exploded. "Painting is my way of being nice to people!"

"Then why are you mad at me?"

"I'm furious at Tahar for what he did. I'm mad at you for not getting it."

"I get it," he insisted.

"Then do something."

"Where is he?"

"In my room."

"Wait here."

"I feel filthy. I'm going upstairs to shower."

Paul advanced along a corridor hung with wrought-iron candleholders shaped like swords, an invitation to arm himself. Had it been any resident other than Tahar, he would have called the police. He considered dialing Spann's cell number but feared that that would put Tahar on the next plane to Guantanamo.

Simone's room was abandoned. A rumpled sheet on the bed resembled something a rural bride might hang in a window on her wedding night. Tahar had ejaculated blood. He hurried to Tahar's door and pounded it with his fist.

"Leave me alone," Tahar shouted.

"You can't treat Simone like that."

"Ask her how she treated me."

"You have to leave."

"Let me finish my work."

Paul hauled at the door handle. It was locked. He tried a master key, but Tahar had shot the inside bolt. The door didn't budge.

"Open up or I'll break it down." This was a futile threat. The stout wood planks, reinforced by brass rivets, would yield to nothing less than a sledge hammer. And what then? Punch the dapper little professor into submission? Drag him bodily out of the *carmen*? "Be sensible," Paul shouted. "Move to a hotel until Spann comes for you."

"Have mercy," Tahar pleaded. "I'm almost at the end. Let me stay for the few days I have left."

After more begging and bargaining, Paul relented. It wasn't simply that Tahar sounded so abject. Paul held out hope—and perhaps Tahar shared that hope—that if he finished his book, Spann might read it and change his mind.

• • •

Wrapped in Paul's robe, Simone sat in a desk chair in the center of the tower, where sunlight cast a pool of warmth that helped dry her hair. When he told her he had agreed to let Tahar stay, she erupted. "That's insane. I won't feel safe till he's gone."

"It's only until the end of the week. He's locked in his room."

"And I'm in my room right down the hall. Put yourself in my place."

"We'll change your room."

"I'll sleep here," she said, "as far from him as possible."

That night, it seemed that Simone also remained as far from Paul as possible. She was there, yet not there, squeezed in beside him on the single bed but absent. Physically and emotionally, she had checked out. In the dead of night, he woke holding his breath, bursting with worry over what came next.

• • •

In the morning, no matter what Paul said, Simone's reply was monosyllabic and a beat slow. Her eyes, which usually possessed submarine depths, now held everything on the surface.

Patsy filled the silence, muttering that life at the *carmen* had become loco. Spewing street Spanish and Portuguese obscenities, she maintained that she had foreseen all this when Tahar had failed to sweep his cut hair from the floor. Now he was under a spell, a curse. Three times a day, she fixed a food tray and placed it on the floor in front of his door. "I feel like I'm feeding an animal in a cage," Patsy fumed.

When Paul translated this for Simone, she said, "That's what he is, an animal."

"At least he's a clean one. I smelled detergent," Patsy said. "He must be washing his clothes before he leaves."

• • •

Paul despaired of getting any rest in the single bed with Simone and so arranged cushions on the floor. She said nothing. Neither did he. On the window ledges, roosting pigeons and doves supplied soothing white noise. Still, he couldn't sleep.

Starting with his father, Paul had hated silent, withholding men. He felt they were judging him, denying him something indefinable that he craved. Now it seemed that he had become a member of that closemouthed tribe—glib enough when nothing was at stake, dead quiet when it counted. There should have been something to say to Simone. An explanation, a promise.

Finally she was the one who spoke. "I told you I left your father right after we returned from the island. But that's not how it happened."

"It doesn't matter," he said.

"It does to me. I was with him until the end."

"The end of what?"

"The end of his life. He was in terrible shape. In bed—"

"I don't want to hear what my father was like in bed."

"Maybe you don't care, but he cared. He was humiliated and enraged. I tried to calm him down and said he should get help. Quit drinking. See a doctor about a prescription for pills. But all he did was get angrier and more withdrawn."

"Is that what you think I'm doing by sleeping on the floor?"

"I know you're not sleeping. Neither am I. I've never told this to anybody. Not even the police after he killed himself."

Paul fumbled in the dark and found her hand. Her palm had the texture of a cat's tongue. He held tight. She didn't squeeze back but accepted the contact as a signal to continue. "He stopped meeting his classes. I told the dean that he was under a doctor's care for depression. He couldn't write, couldn't even read. One day, he was up in his bedroom, and I heard him open the dresser drawer, the one with his guns. He called for me, 'Simone, I need you.'

"I was terrified he'd kill me. But I couldn't *not* go upstairs. He waited until I was in the doorway. Then he put the gun in his mouth, pulled the trigger, and blew off the top of his head."

"Jesus." Paul knelt beside the bed, agonizingly aware that something was required of him. But what? She didn't move. Her hand in his was lifeless. He touched her face. There were no tears.

"I know he blamed me," she said. "He felt it was my fault that he was falling apart. He shot himself to punish me. Calling me up there, near enough to splash blood on me, was part of that punishment."

"He had been on the brink of suicide for years," Paul said and explained that his father had always needed a witness for validation. It was like Tahar and his desire for Simone to paint him and accept him. When he said this, Simone's hand tensed and she attempted to pull away. He tightened his grip.

Anxious to continue talking, he climbed into bed and embraced her. He thought he knew now what had brought her to Granada—the need to share with him what she had witnessed. A need like his father's, not so much for forgiveness as for simple acknowledgment. But Simone said nothing, and in a matter of minutes, she dozed off, her hand in his, twitching as she dreamed.

• • •

The day that Spann arrived to collect Tahar, the Hand of Fatima resounded against the front door like a pistol shot. Paul stepped outside, where Spann was barking orders at a marine in an SUV who was tapping at a cell phone that he held like a vanity mirror close to his face. Spann turned to Paul. "I hate these catch-and-release missions. Like I'm some fucking sports fisherman, reeling them in—which is the fun part—only to toss them back into the mix. I've wasted months of my life for nothing."

"Are you releasing Tahar?" Paul was suffused with hope.

"He's not going to Guantanamo, if that's what you're worried about. He's headed home to Algeria."

"He's been in his room all week, finishing his book. Why not read it before you make up your mind?"

Zipped into his parka, Spann resembled the Michelin Man,

his head stacked atop tires and inner tubes. "I've told you I don't make the rules. I just follow orders."

"Spoken like Adolf Eichmann."

"I love a wiseass. You're the only entertaining part of this detail. It almost breaks my heart to tell you about your father."

"What about him?"

"You asked was he CIA or some type of intelligence agent. Turns out he was on the fringes. Nothing official. He was a wannabe working for chump change. During the '70s, he filed a few reports about suspected leftist subversives."

"Here in Spain?"

"Yeah. When Franco was still more or less alive. After he went back to the States, he stayed active, providing unpaid info about antiwar activists on campus."

"What about assignments in the Caribbean?"

"Not a one. Funny thing is, a legitimate asset in the islands once ran into your old man and suggested we investigate him for impersonating an agent. To put the best spin on it, he was like you—just a good American who volunteered to help Uncle Sam."

"I didn't volunteer," Paul said.

"Let's not fall out over fine distinctions." Spann's chubby cheeks positively beamed.

It infuriated Paul to hear Spann equate him with his father, a pathetic figure, a two-bit informer, like Tahar, with nothing to trade in the end. He wasn't even capable of committing suicide without traumatizing a woman who had obviously loved him.

As they entered the *carmen*, Spann sniffed the air, his nostrils quivering like a rabbit's. "What's that?"

"Patsy's cooking breakfast."

"No. There's a smell of detergent. Ammonia."

"Tahar's washing his clothes."

"I'll fetch the wily oriental gentleman and meet you in a few minutes."

CHAPTER XVII

Blessed stayed alone in the stone hut, praying, starving, cleansing himself, preparing for what lay ahead. Stranded on the quarry's broken rocks, he might have been back in the Sahara, on the reg, a limitless stretch of gravel where a man could be closer to God. Another blank space of the sort that every Believer had to pass through. He surrendered himself to it, like a corpse in the hands of a corpse washer.

Some nights, a membrane covered the moon like a caul on a newborn baby. That was how Blessed had come into this world, marked by an augury of good luck or bad. With no imam to advise him which, he was on his own in an unfathomable universe.

At sunrise, he did what he must, drinking rainwater that had collected in crevasses, brushing his teeth with the *miswah* until his gums bled. At a different puddle, he stripped naked, crouched on his heels, and performed *wudu*, the daily cleaning ritual. At the base of the dead palm tree, he pressed his forehead to the ground and rose with grit spangling his skin.

Plastic bottles and bags and tin cans littered the quarry. In his village, such debris would be valuable. Blessed could carry food in the plastic bags and water in the bottles and shape the tin cans into utensils. With such riches, he could afford to marry and have children.

But how could he feed a family here, where nothing grew? He could barely keep himself alive, eating hard bread handed out of the back doors of bakeries and oranges discarded outside juice shops. He rubbed lemon into his hair, bleaching the tips of his cornrows until they trembled like flames around his head.

In his recollection, the *carmen* was all he had ever known of paradise. His only chance to recover what he had lost was to warn Paul of his danger. Still, Blessed delayed and practiced phrases that slipped through his mind like worry beads through a man's fingers. He started off thinking in the dialect of his village, then worked the words into Arabic and finally into what he hoped was English.

Some nights, he dreamed he was back on the rubber boat, frightened of drowning in the sea between Morocco and Spain. The water rose, and people cried out to Allah and jumped overboard. Mothers flung their babies into the ocean, then dived in after them, vanishing under the waves. Men grappled and fought and clawed at each other, but they disappeared too. Miraculously Blessed had survived.

Now he begged for a second miracle. From the Book, he knew that in the alternation of night and day, there were signs for righteous men. Still, he hesitated and wondered whether it might be too late. Assassins enforcing the fatwa could have reached the *carmen* already and slaughtered everybody.

During a hard rain, a thunderstorm erupted out of season, and lightning sliced the sky into jagged pieces. At daylight, a rainbow appeared, and Blessed seized on this as his sign. He dressed in his cleanest clothes and packed a few belongings in his black plastic bag. He discarded the filthy blanket that he had worn as a winter coat and left it behind along with the lantern and the knife he had stolen from the fish restaurant. If Paul refused to take him back, Blessed didn't want to be tempted to stab him.

At the crest of a slag heap, he swayed on what might have been the rim of a dormant volcano. In the distance, the mountains above the Alhambra looked less substantial than the snow clouds looming above them. He hurried in that direction, shod in a pair of tennis sneakers he had retrieved from a trash bin. Because the shoes were too small, he had broken down their backs and slipped them on like babouches. Their flat soles lisped against the asphalt as he hiked into town with the plastic bag slung over his shoulder.

Sun warmed his face, and wind tumbled his hair to its golden tips. The air smelled of turned earth, and he remembered tending the garden, weeding the strawberry patch, feeding the fish that floated to the surface of the fountain with gulping mouths. He tried not to think of the snake's head he had hacked off.

On Gran Via Colón, pedestrians streamed along the sunny side of the street. After weeks of icy weather, they unbuttoned their overcoats and soaked up warmth. Outside the Italian *gelateria* where Blessed used to beg, people stood in their pooled shadows and licked ice-cream cones.

He started uphill through Little Morocco, where the cobblestones quavered in afternoon light. These alleys were as familiar to him as the veins on the backs of his hands. On every staircase and street, vendors shouted in a mash-up of languages that clashed with the words in Blessed's head. At Placeta de San Jose, he stopped to catch his breath and calm his rioting mind. After weeks of living on the street, he had lost strength and stamina. The Albaicín vibrated like a bell beneath his feet.

Panting, he climbed Calle San Jose, pressing his shoulder against the walls for support, scraping off flakes of white lime. Passersby avoided him as they would a drunk or drug addict. From balconies rose a frenzy of barking dogs, and in a *mashrabiya,* behind the latticework of a harem window, a wrinkled old crone watched until Blessed was safely out of sight.

At Plaza San Miguel Bajo, he paused again, hands on his knees. He thought he might vomit. At café tables, tourists tightened their grips on their purses, afraid that he intended to rob them. Starting off again, he staggered past the church and the underground garage, then up a flight of steps to the brick-paved plaza. The plastic bag had become too heavy and knocked him off stride as he stumbled across the square.

An old couple perched birdlike on one of the concrete benches, their backs to the Alhambra, their faces tilted to the sun. Blessed was tempted to sit down beside them. Better yet, lie down and rest. But he made himself move on to the far edge of Huerta de Carlos, where he leaned forward to gaze down at the *carmen.* His knees buckled, and he braced himself to keep from falling. An SUV, as black as a hearse, was parked in front of the door. Blessed feared he was too late.

Then he spotted a white man behind the SUV's steering wheel, pecking a finger at his palm. He wore a uniform like a soldier or a chauffeur, not an undertaker. Blessed scrambled down to the *carmen* and banged the heavy Hand of Fatima against the door, shouting, "Danger! Paul, danger!"

The driver bolted out of the SUV. A pistol, a Taser, and a cell phone flapped from his belt. "What the hell do you want?"

The question came to Blessed not as individual words but as a splurge of unintelligible sound. He never stopped slamming the door knocker.

"Put that bag down and grab the wall," the soldier said.

When Blessed didn't comply, he pulled out his phone, not the pistol or Taser. "We got a situation out here. A Black guy's trying to break into the house. Request permission to neutralize him."

CHAPTER XVIII

Paul waited in the kitchen, where Simone was stirring sugar into her coffee. She wore her Fair Isle sweater, as if she intended to suggest another excursion into the country.

"Spann's about to bring Tahar out," Paul said.

She lazily cut her eyes in his direction.

"I thought you'd rather not be around," he said.

"I'm a big girl."

At the stove, Patsy kept watch, tracking every move, every remark, even those she couldn't understand.

Spann breezed in alone, declaiming in a theatrical British accent, "His nibs requested another minute to complete his toilet. How about some coffee? Just a splash. No milk, no sugar."

"Have you heard what Tahar did to me?" Simone asked.

"Nope." Spann lost the accent and collapsed onto a cane-bottom chair that creaked under his weight.

"He assaulted me sexually."

"Your paintings probably turned him on."

"You've been in my room." It sounded like an accusation, not a question. In either case, Spann didn't respond.

Tahar entered the kitchen, carrying the suitcase and overnight bag he had arrived with. He wore the same check cashmere sport coat, the same corduroy trousers and tasseled loafers. But he didn't look the same. He wore a bulky sweater beneath his jacket, and he waddled like a penguin, cautiously picking up and putting down his feet. He set his luggage on the floor and squared his shoulders.

"Don't get comfortable," Spann said. "We're about to saddle up."

After days indoors, Tahar had a slight prison pallor. "Isn't it customary for the condemned man to be allowed a last statement?"

"Keep it short," Spann said.

"Did you finish your book?" Paul asked.

"Yes, I'm finished."

"At least look at it," Paul appealed to Spann, "before you move him out."

"Don't start that again."

For an instant, silence guttered around them. There was only the pulse of electrical appliances. "Early on, I should have known it was already too late for me," Tahar said.

"And getting later all the time," Spann said.

"For Christ's sake, give the guy a break," Paul said.

"No matter how far you fall in this world," Tahar said, "there is no bottom. You can't choose where you land, but you can decide how you end. Many consider life a path to death. I have chosen death as a path to life."

"What is this happy horseshit?" Spann stepped toward Tahar but stopped short when his cell phone rang. Tahar clutched his chest as if the ringing were inside him.

"Tase him and take him down," Spann shouted into the phone.

"I'm on my way." He bolted around a corner down the front hall.

"Are you okay?" Paul asked Tahar.

"Fine." Tahar's hand hadn't moved from his heart. He looked like he was suffering angina.

"Do you need a doctor?" Paul asked.

"It's too late for what I need."

Paul pulled an envelope from his pocket. After a moment's hesitation, Tahar accepted it in his free hand and thumbed it open. Hundred-dollar bills fluttered to the scarred surface of the table.

"Money to help you get started," Paul said.

"I'm not starting. I'm ending."

"But with cash, maybe you can bribe somebody in Algeria and buy a ticket out."

"Too late," Tahar repeated. Tears trickled down his sun-damaged cheeks as he wavered there, an exile, an alien even to himself. Abandoning the money and his bags, he headed in the direction Spann had gone.

Patsy gabbled that if the Arab didn't want the dollars, she did. She scooped up the bills like a croupier.

• • •

Spann blocked the open doorway, hollering orders at the marine. Blessed lay prone on the ground beside the SUV, his wrists flex-cuffed behind his back. The marine had ripped open his plastic bag and was flinging clothes into the road. "He seems to be clean."

"Fuck 'seems,'" Spann hollered. "Make sure!"

Then he heard footsteps behind him. Spann swung around, and the massive door shut at his back. The sound of its slamming was lost in a blast he never heard. The explosion blew out his eardrums. Ex-votos scythed off the walls, dicing his flesh, but he felt nothing. The aftershock sucked the eyes from his skull, and in an instant of white, annihilating heat, the *carmen* flipped upside down and deposited him on the ceiling.

In the kitchen, the table was swept clean of cups and utensils. Splinters of window glass flashed through the grillwork into the garden. Pots and pans spun off the walls and bounced crazily around the room. Simone huddled on the floor next to Patsy, both of them hugging their knees.

Paul checked that they weren't hurt, then hurried into the front hall. Through a red mist, Patsy dogged his heels. Blood and bone splinters sleeted from the ceiling. She flapped her hands as if at stinging hornets and ran back to the kitchen.

At first, Paul noticed no body parts larger than fingers and a single foot laced into a shoe. Then he spotted a head, mangled and unrecognizable, smashed to a roof beam. Brass rivets and flanges held the front door intact, but the detonation had lifted it off its hinges, and it now stretched like a handicap ramp from the top step to the road. The side of the SUV was flecked with torn flesh. A second head, Tahar's, had splattered against the bulletproof windshield. Snowy feathers from Spann's ski parka eddied in the air.

Blessed, still handcuffed, was struggling to stand up. The marine frantically pecked at his phone. When Paul, drenched in blood mist, passed into his field of vision, the marine quit texting. "Are you wounded, sir?"

Paul shook his head and helped Blessed to his feet. He unfastened the flex cuffs, and Blessed embraced him, babbling about danger. As squad cars beetled through the maze of the Albaicín, their sirens rose and fell, rose and fell until they blended into a single blaring noise that could no longer be heard, only felt as a throb in the veins.

"Go," he screamed at Blessed. "Run." Because Blessed was Black, because he had blundered along at the worst moment, Paul was positive he'd be blamed. He shoved him toward the hidden path to San Miguel Bajo.

Brandishing his Taser, the marine said, "Freeze! Both of you down on your bellies." He planted a knee on Blessed's spine and cuffed him again. He did the same to Paul.

"This is my house," Paul protested.

"You told him to run. I heard you."

Guardia Civil cars rumbled down the cobblestone street and bumped to a stop behind the SUV. Men piled out, glanced at the *carmen*'s front door lolling like a tongue from a bloody mouth, then noticed the head on the windshield and fell back. An officer ordered the marine to holster his Taser. He did as instructed but refused when ordered to hit the ground next to Blessed and Paul. "I'm with the US Embassy," he said in English. "Here taking custody of a terrorist."

The Guardia Civil shoved the marine to his knees.

"I can explain," Paul called out in Spanish.

An officer dragged him to a sitting position and propped him against the *carmen*. Atop the retaining wall around his childhood soccer pitch, a crowd stared down at him in stupefaction.

"The Black guy," the Marine blurted, "banged on the door like he was signaling somebody inside."

"He had nothing to do with any of this," Paul said.

The Spanish officer told them both to shut up and asked Paul, "Is anyone in the *carmen*?"

"Two women."

"Are they armed?"

"No."

More squad cars nosed down the narrow road, and cops unspooled yellow crime-scene tape around the perimeter. Two men dressed in helmets and heavy-gauge tunics clipped on clear plastic face shields. Like beekeepers confronting a murderous swarm, they moved tentatively into the *carmen*.

The marine shouted to be heard over the chaos. "The embassy is choppering in a team."

The bomb squad led out Simone and Patsy, who looked like they had red capes draped over their shoulders. The hallway ceiling was still bleeding.

Patsy resisted the Guardia Civil at every step. "Get your hands off me. I'm not your whore."

They flex-cuffed her and slammed her against the wall beside Paul. Then they lowered Simone on the other side.

"Don't tell them anything," Paul whispered. "Not a word. Let me do the talking."

The bomb squad reentered the building with a sniffer dog and a small remote-control robot which preceded them around a corner into the kitchen. It triggered an explosion, barely powerful enough to break open Tahar's bags and prove they didn't contain bombs, just a torrent of ripped pages and note cards.

At the approach of a US helicopter, the crowd reacted in herd panic. The clatter of whirling blades first drove people together and then drove them apart. Some fled across the plaza. Simone quit whimpering and hugged Paul in relief. He didn't share her sense that they had been saved.

The instant its blades stopped spinning, three men vaulted from the chopper. They looked interchangeable—well barbered, flat-bellied, each in a white shirt and tie. They treated the Spanish with chilly correctness, speaking in Castilian accents that prompted immediate pushback from the Andalusians. The Guardia Civil insisted that it retained jurisdiction. The US agents argued that since a State Department official had died during the detention of an Islamic radical, the protocols of the Gobal War on Terror took precedence. After a great deal of palaver, neither side could agree on what those protocols were.

"We're American citizens," Paul shouted.

"The Black guy's not an American." Down in the dirt, the marine objected again to being grouped with the suspects.

Spanish police and US Embassy officials compromised on a division of labor. A local forensic team began to process the scene, collecting the two heads, the fingers, and the shod foot. Then they focused on bone fragments and cloth fibers, working with trowels and tweezers, brushes and specimen bags.

Meanwhile, American officials attended to the people still cuffed on the ground. Simone was sobbing, and they handled her gently. Patsy bridled when they patted her down and protested that she was being treated like a whore. They freed the marine, then ordered him to release Paul.

"Now uncuff Blessed," Paul said. "He's not involved in this. He was just passing by."

"Hold it a second," the marine piped up. "I heard him tell the Black guy to leave the scene."

"Blessed doesn't know anything," Paul said.

The American who did most of the talking gestured for the marine to unfasten the plastic flex from Blessed's wrists. "These women, who are they?" he asked Paul.

"One's the cook. The other's an artist. A guest at the residency."

Patsy insisted that she could damn well speak for herself, while Simone sank into a silence so deep she might have been in a trance.

"Spann described this as some sort of arts colony," the US official said.

"Right," Paul answered. "He claimed to be with the State Department and asked me to let Tahar finish a book here. He never warned me he was dangerous. He damn well should have. Now my business, my house, is ruined."

The sky had clouded over, and the temperature was falling. Simone started to shiver. The Guardia Civil announced that it was going to seal the *carmen*. Before it did so, Paul protested that he had to retrieve a few things from inside.

"I want to go home." Simone spoke for the first time.

"Sorry. You'll have to stay in custody. Protective custody," the American explained.

"You're arresting us? On what charge?" Paul demanded.

"No charge. We're holding you in a hotel until we sort the situation."

Patsy protested that she had her own apartment and browbeat the Americans into sending her home with an escort to stand guard. Blessed fell into an altogether different category—the penniless Black African migrant category. The Spanish preferred to jail him. The Americans didn't disagree. But Paul spoke up against slamming Blessed into a cell while Simone and he stayed at a hotel.

"Have it your way." The US officer cracked a smile, showing off his excellent orthodonture. "Bunk in the same room with him for all I care."

As Paul returned to the *carmen,* his numb shock drained away, replaced by fear and revulsion. The ceiling had stopped drizzling blood, but he could smell it, he could taste it in the air. The hallway tiles were sticky and sucked at his shoes. The walls were like a cattle chute, streaked with horn gouges. On the staircase to the tower, he left a trail of red prints, fainter at each step. By the time he reached the top, his feet barely made a mark.

The windows were spiderwebbed with cracks, and through jagged glass, he gazed down at the scrum of Guardia Civil and US agents around the SUV. A few onlookers had crept back and lined the retaining wall beneath a bruised purple sky.

Paul stripped to his bare, clammy skin, dried off with the bedsheet, and changed into clean clothes. He had hidden Spann's money under the floorboards and had folded some bills into reference books. He retrieved and divided the cash into separate wads that he wedged into his pockets. Then he went back downstairs.

• • •

In spite of the rain, the Spaniards and Americans lingered, discussing plans. The Guardia Civil volunteered to transfer Paul, Simone, and Blessed to a hotel. The Americans would follow in a second squad car and post guards outside their rooms. A clap of thunder finally cut the discussion short.

Ankle-deep water spilled down the streets, and the squad car drenched pedestrians as it splashed past. Shopkeepers rang down their shutters; blind lottery-ticket vendors sheltered in doorways. Simone slumped against Paul, rubbing the sleeve of his shirt between her fingers. On the other side, Blessed sat rigidly upright, his plastic bag of clothes balanced on his knees.

Paseo de los Tristes streamed along beside the crackling bed of the Darro River. The Guardia Civil paused at a hotel and dropped off its passengers. Then the American officials handled the check-in formalities, guaranteeing payment with a US government–issued credit card. When the concierge booked Simone and Paul into the same room, Paul explained that the señorita would occupy a single, while he and Blessed took a double with twin beds.

"Put them on the same floor," the US agent instructed the concierge. Then, to Paul, "This way one guard can cover all three of you."

In a wood-paneled elevator as cramped and airless as a coffin, Simone nestled against Paul, just as she had at night in the tower's narrow bed. Next to one another, yet not actually together. They parted at her room, and she glanced back at him, waiflike, distressed. Again, it seemed that she expected more of him. There was so much he felt he should say, but not with the guard hovering behind them.

In the other room, Blessed circled like a dog deciding where to settle. Paul gestured to a bed and said, "Yours." He showed him the minibar stuffed with snacks and encouraged him to eat whatever he wanted. Then, in the bathroom, he demonstrated how to switch on the shower and adjust the temperature. Blessed gave him a look. Paul was overdoing it; he'd figure things out for himself.

At the front window, Paul watched the rain purl along the riverbanks. Bare tree branches drooped over the Darro, beating at a frothing current treacherous enough to drown a man. Or a little boy. Paul buried that thought and stared off at the statue of the celebrated dead flamenco dancer, Mario Maya.

He regretted that he had never seen Maya perform. He regretted that he had never danced with Simone, had never even listened to music with her. He had many regrets, large and small, and tried to hide behind them now and evade the gruesome memories of the day.

There was a knock at the door. Simone with the guard. She had showered and smelled of shampoo yet still wore the bloodstained Fair Isle sweater. "I should have asked you to bring some clothes for me to change into. Do you have a shirt I could borrow?"

He told her he did, and when he brought it, she said, "I'm hungry. Can you call down and have them send up some food?"

"What would you like?"

"Soup and bread and cheese sounds nice. And wine. Enough for the two of us."

"Blessed's in the shower," Paul said. "When he's finished, I'll see what he wants."

She extended a tentative hand that didn't quite touch him. "I was hoping we could spend some time together." Then she added, "You saved my life," and did touch him.

Paul ordered food for Blessed and two meals to be delivered next door. As an afterthought, he asked if the guard wanted anything to eat, and the fellow in his suit and starched shirt and tie said he didn't.

Once they were alone, Simone pulled off her sweater and tossed it on the floor in a far corner of the room. She wore a pastel-pink bra. She shed it too and threw it into the same corner. After bundling up in Paul's shirt, she unfolded a bath towel and mimed for him to bend down so she could wipe the blood from his hair.

He shied away. "I'm okay."

"You could shower here."

"I'm okay," he repeated, settling onto a spindly chair at a faux-antique desk.

Simone settled against the headboard of the bed. "I must look awful."

"You look fine."

"I don't feel fine. But this shirt smells like you, and that lifts my spirits."

She had gone from mute incomprehension to nervous chatter, like a battlefield survivor. She insisted on recalling events as if Paul hadn't witnessed them himself. Where survival made Simone giddy, Paul was driven deeper into himself. When she repeated that he had saved her life, he still didn't reply. "I think

Tahar meant to kill us all," she said. "But then you were kind to him and offered to call a doctor, and you gave him some money. That must have changed his mind, and he decided he'd only kill Spann."

A bellboy brought cheese and sausage, bowls of soup, and a couple of crescent rolls—*medialunas* left over from breakfast. The boy uncorked a bottle of red, poured two glasses, and departed with a worried glance at Paul's bloody head.

Simone patted the bed beside her. Paul stayed in the chair and arranged his wine on the desk precisely atop the circular stain from a previous glass. "Blessed's the one who saved us," he said, "when he banged on the door, and Spann went to find out what was wrong."

"Whatever," Simone said. "We were damn lucky." Paul let this pass. "You don't appear to think so."

"Lucky is the last thing I feel."

"Why do I get the impression you blame me?"

"I blame myself. I should never have let Tahar live at the *carmen.* But it seemed to me a chance to help a man in trouble. To give a hand to a migrant. And to make some money," he admitted.

"You should have kicked him out when I asked you to." She swallowed a spoonful of soup and frowned. "It's cold."

Paul started to sip his wine but stopped before the glass touched his lips. He placed it back on the stain. "The Spanish and the Americans are bound to ask questions about you and me and our relationship. You'd be smart to distance yourself. Especially if they charge me."

"Charge you with what?"

"They have a long list to choose from. Americans have a nasty habit of treating witnesses to terrorism as accessories or accomplices. You don't want to get mixed up in that."

"But I am a witness. What am I supposed to do—perjure myself?"

"That's not what I meant. Just, you know, keep some space between us."

"Is that what you're doing now? Sitting across the room? Not even looking at me? Should I assume this is to protect me?"

"Why don't you assume," he said, "that two men were just blown to bits in my house. Assume I'm having a hard time processing it. Assume if we don't play our cards right, I could lose the *carmen* and land in jail."

Simone waited for him to go on.

"It's up to you what you care to tell them about Tahar," he resumed. "But you say the wrong thing, and you could come in for a rough interrogation."

"They'll see I was painting Tahar."

"Fine. Stick to art. He was your model. One of many. No different from the men on Random Chat."

"Chat Random," she corrected him.

"You know what I mean," he said, peeved at her punctiliousness. "Don't mention that he hit on you. Or that the two of you argued and you encouraged me to kick him out."

"Who am I protecting here?" she asked again.

"You're protecting yourself."

"Against what?"

"Against people putting their own spin on the story."

"You've lost me."

"Look, Simone, step back and see things from the other side. Both the Americans and the Spanish might decide to deny that this was a terrorist incident. It could be to their advantage to pass it off as a spat between a painter and a sexually frustrated Algerian who turned suicidal when he got rejected."

"So we're back to blaming me. Like I was the one who made Tahar into a suicide bomber."

"We're trying to make sure nobody blames you."

"But you consider it plausible, don't you?"

"Jesus, we're going in circles."

"What if what I want is to tell them that I came to Granada out of curiosity, on a lark, to get a new perspective on my life? Then I fell in love with you. What if I say Tahar was jealous and decided to kill us?"

There was terrific emotion in her voice, but no tenderness. "My brain is fried," Paul said. "I can't keep fighting you on this."

He crossed the room and kissed Simone on the cheek. Slipping a hand behind his head, she started to ease him down beside her. But her fingers snagged in his bloody hair, and they both pulled back.

• • •

Blessed was in bed with a towel around his waist and a food tray on his lap. His body resembled a bundle of sticks whittled out of ebony, each rib, each bone and joint in high relief. His skin didn't seem to fit him. There were wrinkles at the crooks of his arms and the backs of his knees. He had devoured the carry-out dinner and emptied the minibar and was now swigging a Diet Pepsi and munching salted cashews from a can.

"If you're hungry, I'll order more," Paul said.

"No. Tired now."

Outside the window, rain slanted past the streetlamps in gray pencil strokes. A bus hydroplaned around a corner, skidding toward Sacramonte. The ceiling light and the minibar hummed. Or was that the blood in Paul's brain? Of all the day's shocks, Simone's declaration, spoken in anger, that she had fallen in love with him nagged at Paul. Why had she waited this long to say so? Was it the same reason she had waited to tell him she had slept with his father?

"I have a thing to say," Blessed broke in. "The man with his head on the car, I can never forget."

"No. I can't either. I'm going to shower, then sleep."

• • •

Blood rinsed from Paul's hair in a mist that called to mind the hallway and the hellish baptism he had undergone—not so much reborn as bumbling into a new life that would never be the same. Dying the way they had, reduced to shreds, Spann and Tahar, he thought, would remain with him forever.

When he stepped out of the bathroom, he almost tripped over Blessed, who was crouched on the floor, whispering *isha*, the night prayer. Paul backed off and let him finish, and when he came out a second time, Blessed was in bed under the covers.

The two of them lay in darkness, weighed down by all the

words they weren't able to express. The silence, the separate beds, the guilt he suffered reminded Paul of the anguished dissolution of many an old love affair. For a time, he was tempted to switch to Simone's room. But the distance between here and there struck him at this hour as unbridgeable.

"You pray," Blessed said.

To Paul, this sounded like an admonishment, a command. It took him an instant to realize it was a question. "Yes. In my own way, I do."

"Tell me your way."

It was too late and Paul was too tired to admit that he had no way. "We'll talk another time."

CHAPTER XIX

For a week afterward, Paul woke each day from a coma of nightmares—none of whose details he recalled but that nevertheless steeped him in dread. He sensed the city shuddering around him, as if he had fallen from a great height and shattered. He remembered feeling this way as a kid—that everything he loved could be lost in an instant, that he could not only be killed but scattered in tiny pieces. Virtudes's violent Civil War stories had stoked this fear, as had visits with his father, when every inadvertent error on his part threatened severe punishment.

Yet nothing that followed the suicide blast was as catastrophic as he expected. He, Simone, and Blessed stayed under guard in their hotel rooms, but the Spanish authorities showed little enthusiasm for any investigation. The three of them went through desultory questioning, then signed sworn statements that made no effort to iron out contradictions. The local press carried a bare-bones account of the incident that sounded like a rerun of dozens of previous terrorist attacks. Tahar was described as an Algerian radical, suspected of ties to ISIS and AQIM. "A lone-wolf terrorist," every article emphasized. He was said to have applied for asylum in the United States and been rejected. Rather than accept repatriation, Tahar Mahmoud had committed suicide and in the process caused the death of a US national. Due to security accords between the United States and Spain, the dead man's identity wasn't revealed.

In the States, wire services recycled stories by Spanish journalists, adding Spann's name but no information about his intelligence affiliation. They referred to the crime scene as an arts colony where a noted American painter had barely escaped injury. An unnamed source—Paul suspected this must be Patsy—had revealed that Mahmoud had posed nude for Simone Pierce. Although the mainstream press didn't reproduce samples of her work, the weedy fringes of the Internet provided multiple illustrations, some uncensored, others with gray blobs superimposed over the genitals of models.

One American magazine carried what purported to be an exclusive interview with Simone Pierce. It quoted her defense of herself against accusations of pornography. She argued that she was part of a tradition as ancient as art itself. She mentioned cave drawings and primitive statues of fertility gods and goddesses that were every bit as explicit as her work. Courbet, Schiele, and Picasso, she said, had prefigured contemporary female artists who validated the penis and the vagina as worthy subjects for aesthetic exploration.

All of these quotations, it eventually came out, had been lifted from a profile of Simone published a decade ago in a catalogue raisonné.

• • •

When Paul felt that enough time had passed and he could cope with his emotions, he requested permission to return to the *carmen.* American officials murmured about "an ongoing process" and "a few final steps" that needed to be completed first. They invited him to a breakfast meeting in the hotel dining room, a stripped-down functional space, uncrowded in this season and overstocked with a buffet of Serrano ham and Manchego cheese, hard-boiled eggs, and yogurt. Two men from the State Department served themselves a bit of everything, piling their plates high. Given their appetites, Paul thought they should have been the size of Bill Spann. But in every respect, they were his obverse—athletically trim, soft-spoken, and polite.

Paul ordered a coffee, which was delivered by a uniformed waiter who drizzled a brown-sugar line drawing of the Alhambra over its milky surface. The Americans handed Paul their cards. One was named Doug, the other Emerson. Doug did most of the talking while Emerson tossed his tie back over his shoulder to keep it out of his food and thumbed notes into a smart phone.

"I don't know how much Bill Spann told you," Doug started.

"Very little. Obviously not enough."

"He must have said something to persuade you to let Mahmoud live at your place."

"Didn't Spann discuss that in his notes?" Paul asked.

"We'd rather hear your version."

"I'd like to hear Spann's."

"Sorry. That's classified."

Paul chuckled. "This is sort of one-way traffic, isn't it? It's simple from my side. Spann showed up at the *carmen* like a door-to-door salesman and said the State Department needed to debrief an Algerian asylum seeker. He was a writer who would fit in at an arts residency. Spann appealed to my patriotism, then sweetened the deal by offering money." Paul sipped his coffee, shifting the sugary outline of the Alhambra. "But first, I had to clear out other people."

"Ms. Pierce didn't clear out." A talented multitasker, Doug ate as he talked.

"Spann agreed she could stay."

"And that was important to you. Why?"

"I'd ask you the same question. Why's that important?"

"Just getting facts straight."

"I'm sure Spann reported that she and I were sleeping together. He wouldn't have ignored something like that. What upsets me is how little warning he thought to give me about Tahar."

"He told you there was a fatwa against Mahmoud. It's in his notes."

"But the fatwa had nothing to do with what happened. Tahar acted on his own for reasons that had no connection to what some imam supposedly said. In fact, Spann told me you guys knew Tahar had posted the fatwa himself."

"So what's your best guess why Mahmoud blew up Spann and himself?"

"Did you know Spann personally? How much time did you spend around him?"

"Enough to get an impression."

"Then you know how abrasive he could be. The kind of guy

who thought he was funny. He seemed to get off on rubbing people the wrong way. I'm sure there were no grace notes when he rejected Tahar for asylum."

"Spann doesn't call the shots on who's approved and who isn't."

"Okay, he was just the messenger boy for whoever makes the decisions. But he was the one who was here when Tahar put on a suicide vest."

"The way you talk, Spann turned Mahmoud into a terrorist."

"I don't blame it all on him. There's more than enough to go around. What concerns me is what the US means to do about my home."

"We're prepared to discuss damages once we clarify a few points."

Paul digested this along with the last of his coffee.

"Did Tahar have a cell phone?" Doug asked.

"Not that I ever noticed."

"What about the landline at your place; did he use it?"

"There's no landline. With so many residents in and out, I had it disconnected years ago. It was costing me a fortune in international calls."

"Did he ever discuss his Internet searches?"

"No."

"Did he ever talk about bomb-making?"

"No."

"Did he ever express extremist views?"

"About what?"

Emerson had trouble transcribing Doug's rapid-fire questions. Doug noticed this and slowed down. "About politics? Islam? Terror tactics? US policy?"

"Tahar was a knowledgeable guy. An academic full of opinions. During his months here, he talked about a lot of subjects. But never anything that made me suspect he planned to set off a bomb. His obsession was relocating to the States."

"How do you figure his posing for Ms. Pierce fits in?"

"I don't believe it has any relevance at all. What artists do in their studios is their business, not mine."

"But you and she were intimate? She must have said something about him."

"We had better things to talk about than Tahar. She used a bunch of different models. We didn't discuss any of them."

"In the end," Doug said, "Spann recommended renditioning Mahmoud for enhanced interrogation. People in Washington overruled Spann and decided it was safe to repatriate him. Now those people's asses are on the line."

"Pardon me for not sympathizing with them. My sympathy is with Tahar for believing he had to lie to save his life. For committing suicide to keep from being tortured again."

"You're wasting your sympathy on him. It's just dumb luck he didn't kill you and everyone else. Obviously he had access to bomb-making materials at your place."

"I don't know anything about bomb-making."

"He could have assembled a suicide vest from household products."

"Look, you're telling me stuff I don't know anything about. I'd like to help you, but I've got enough trouble worrying about where I'm going to live, how I'm going to live." He clacked his coffee cup down onto the saucer.

"Okay, we'll discuss compensation. But not here," Doug

said. "We'll do that after we've walked through your property."

In a hard-bodied Chevy SUV with CD plates, they barged through the Albaicín's warren of streets. The massive tires screamed at every intersection. Paul sensed that they were going too fast. Pedestrians flattened themselves against walls. Stray dogs and cats scrambled to safety.

At the *carmen*, a temporary front door had been fashioned out of a sheet of plywood. It looked much too flimsy to deter thieves. Despite crime-scene tape that still cordoned off the area, graffiti artists had sneaked in and tagged the plywood with gang signs and team logos. The doorframe, bloodstained around its edges, resembled a mouth that had taken a savage punch.

"Claims adjusters already did a walk-through and worked up some numbers." From his briefcase, Doug extracted a blueprint of the *carmen* that showed the blast damage room by room. "Keep this copy for your records. You can consult it as we check things out. If you notice something we missed, give a shout."

Emerson stepped aside while Doug yanked loose the plywood, releasing a cold, sour exhalation from the hallway. High-powered hoses had scoured away the blood, leaving the whitewashed walls rose-tinted. At ground zero, cracked tiles grated underfoot. They might have been treading on splintered teeth, shuffling through mangled ex-votos that rattled like discarded tin cans. Paul had feared that the *carmen* would reek of death. Instead, there was a pervasive smell of disinfectant. Only Tahar's suite had a distinctly different odor—of bleach, ammonia, and fingernail-polish remover.

"I have a hard time understanding how Tahar improvised a bomb that would do this much damage," Paul said.

"During the evacuation of Afghanistan," Doug said, "a terrorist in a suicide vest killed over a hundred and eighty people at Kabul Airport."

In the library, window glass glinted on the furniture, and torn pages and book covers papered the floor. A couple of pots and pans still dangled from pegs above the kitchen sink. But every dish and cup, every hand-fired piece of Moroccan ceramic, was in shards.

Doug pointed out cracks in the masonry and remarked that an architect would have to determine which walls were load bearing and should be reinforced. "In the States," he said, "a homeowner would probably tear the house down and start over."

"The Albaicín is a UNESCO Heritage Site," Paul said. "Nothing can be changed."

But for him, everything had already changed. Heartsick, he took consolation that neither his mother nor Virtudes had lived to see the *carmen* in this condition.

In Simone's studio, watercolors had peeled off the walls, as tightly rolled as old diplomas. The oil paintings had toppled from their easels. Paul flipped one right side up, revealing a luridly colored vulva. Doug's only comment was "Should Ms. Pierce choose to file a claim, it'll have to be separate from yours."

On the stairs to the tower, Paul's bloody footprints remained visible as dull brown smudges, and he experienced a minor chord of the major trauma he had suffered the day Tahar and Spann had died. Not just died, been obliterated.

The querencia where he had spent so many hours nestled in the safety of Virtudes's lap was now a squawking aviary. Birds had stolen in through the shattered windows and roosted on his desk and bed. Acid white droppings encrusted the computer lid and spangled the floor. When the birds spotted the three men, they boiled up in a swarm, orbited the tower in instinctive order, and rushed outside, their wings scissoring the sky.

The flowing beauty of their flight raised Paul's gaze above the Alhambra's afternoon glory all the way to the snowcapped Sierra Madre. At least some things were the same, and this gave him hope that he could recover. The tower had been bombarded by Franco's troops and then rebuilt. He saw no reason why that couldn't be done again.

They descended the stairs, Doug first, then Paul, then Emerson, pecking at his phone. "I assume you have insurance," Doug said.

"Nothing that'll cover all my losses."

"Do you have a number in mind?" On the ground floor, Doug paused to catch his breath and for Emerson to catch up with his transcription. "A ballpark figure that'll make you whole," Doug added, as if it were Paul who had been blown apart.

"The *carmen*'s been in my family for generations," Paul said. "Its foundations go back before Islamic times to the Roman era. My mother's mother's mother's father bought it as a ruin and reconstructed it."

"We understand you have sentimental attachments."

"Not just that. They don't build *carmens* these days. The art and the antiques had actual value." Paul feared he sounded like a rug merchant in Little Morocco. "Make me an offer."

"If you're looking for a global settlement, we'd need a global agreement. In exchange for waiving your rights to all claims, present and future, we're prepared to indemnify you against the cost of repairs and replacements on a fair-value basis to be determined by independent appraisal."

"I asked you to make an offer. You're quoting me legal boilerplate."

"Well, we're talking about a binding contract to cover all tangible losses."

"Not all my losses are tangible. And there's the income I'll lose while the *carmen*'s being repaired. I may never be able to operate it as an arts residency again. Who'll want to come here after what happened?"

"We'd of course factor in collateral costs. That's what the arbitration process is for."

"Arbitration process?" Paul exaggerated his annoyance. "Is that what we're doing? Starting a process that'll probably drag on until I'm an old man? I'm expecting punitive damages."

"The State Department has guidelines. Congressional oversight committees that'll want to have a say."

"Where were those oversight committees when you put a suicide bomber in my home and he destroyed it?"

"Be reasonable. Compensation requires congressional approval, and appropriation bills need to—"

"There are other kinds of bills," Paul broke in. "Dollar bills that don't show up in congressional budgets. They're shrink-wrapped in plastic. I'm talking about the kind of cash you people airdropped into Iraq and Afghanistan to pay off warlords and politicians."

Doug looked terribly disappointed in Paul. "Is that what you want?"

"That's exactly what I want. And one more thing. Blessed, he needs papers to stay in Spain. I'm sure you can arrange that."

"And in return, you're willing to sign a confidentiality agreement?"

"Yes. For that and a serious amount of money!"

CHAPTER XX

Simone refused to return to the *carmen*. Nothing Paul said could change her mind. It didn't make any difference that all traces of the bombing had been scrubbed clean and the walls replastered. She told him that she'd rather abandon her belongings, including her paintings, than walk down the hallway where, she believed, atoms of the dead men polluted the air.

In the end, he packed her clothes into her Louis Vuitton suitcases and transported them to the hotel. Then he hired a shipping agent to roll her watercolors into cardboard tubes and hammer together crates for the oil paintings. Simone instructed that they be dispatched to her gallery in New York City.

• • •

At the *carmen*, a construction crew hung a new front door, gleaming with brass rivets and hinges. Then glaziers replaced the broken glass. Rather than duplicate the wooden frames and mullioned panes that had been flecked with bubbles like eye floaters, Paul ordered double-glazed windows and draft-proof aluminum fittings. That minor upgrade seemed to liberate him for larger ones. As the reconstruction continued, he tossed out the dark, overstuffed furniture from the library and the studios in favor of lighter and brighter sofas and chairs, which, if not entirely up-to-date, were at least of the current century. Rather than shop in antique stores for copies of the original ex-votos and wrought-iron lamp fixtures, he installed track lighting and bright posters.

He urged Blessed to move back in and offered him his pick of rooms. Blessed chose the kitchen supply closet and couldn't be dissuaded from settling there. In return for the visa that Paul had arranged for him, Blessed said he'd work for free. Paul wouldn't hear of it and paid him to join the construction crew during the day and guard the house at night. Blessed bragged of his security prowess at the rock quarry and promised to keep an eye on the laborers, most of whom were African migrants. It wasn't long before Paul noticed that growing numbers of these migrants had spread bedrolls in the courtyard. In foul weather, they moved inside the *carmen*.

"They have no other safe place to sleep," Blessed explained.

"Doesn't the construction company pay them?"

"Not enough."

"What happens when the job's finished?"

"They go."

"Where?"

Blessed lifted his bony shoulders and let them sag. "No one knows. Here they can cook and come to no harm. For them, it's paradise."

"And for you?" Paul asked.

"The same."

When Paul inquired about Patsy, Blessed answered with another shrug. Apparently she had flown home to Cape Verde with the money she'd scooped up in the kitchen.

• • •

The State Department cancelled the guard in the corridor, but it continued to cover the hotel bill. Simone and Paul came and went as they pleased but rarely visited each other's rooms, and they never spent the night together. Usually at the end of an affair, Paul was eager to flee; he preferred to lick his wounds in private. Now, to his surprise, he was content to meet Simone each morning for breakfast and dawdle over cups of coffee, the two of them swept up in a conversation that mostly swam around their heads and only occasionally emerged in words. Where this nontalk was taking them he had no idea. Perhaps Simone did. He was aware only that a current—was it desire?—vibrated between them. Finally he told her, "I don't want this to end."

"Breakfast?"

"You know that's not what I mean."

"As a matter of fact, I don't know what you mean. You haven't been very communicative."

"I'd like us to try again."

"Try what? I can't remember the last time you even touched me."

"Sure, you can remember. A couple of weeks ago, in bed, in the tower."

"So you're saying try sex again?" She flashed a provocative grin.

"That might be a good start. Then I'd like you to move back in and take a chance at working things out long term."

"You know how I feel about your place."

"It's not the same place. It's being completely redone. You could help decorate it."

"I'm a painter. Not an interior decorator."

"Fine. Fix a studio for yourself and paint."

She stirred her coffee. "Then what? Become a permanent resident and paying guest?"

"Let's quit doing this—trading wisecracks. After what we've been through, I think we owe each other more than that."

The grin faded into her tough-girl face. "You've left this a little late, haven't you?"

"You waited till the day Tahar and Spann died to say you had fallen in love with me."

She sighed. "Don't quote me on that. I wasn't in my right mind."

"So you haven't fallen for me?"

"Oh, head over heels." The throwaway line was double-edged, ironic and sincere at the same time.

"Then why not stay?"

"My career, my life is in the States. How would you feel about relocating to New York City?"

Paul wasn't sure of the seriousness of her question. "You told me the advantage of the Internet was that you can paint anyplace. My life is in Granada."

"In one tiny corner of Granada. In a house that's haunted for me. I know how to compete with another woman. How can I compete with the Albaicín? Do you plan on hiding here forever?"

He drew back in protest. "How can you accuse me of hiding? I opened my house to all comers, and the whole world crashed down on me. You didn't have any trouble finding me."

"Okay, and I'm glad I did. I hope it brought both of us closure."

"Not me. I'm wide open. Ready for what's next." He reached across the table and held her hands, which, now that she didn't scour them with solvents, had lost their emery-board abrasiveness.

"Look, New York is only eight hours away," she said. "Why don't we enjoy one of those intense international relationships? And until I leave, we don't have to be strangers. Some people believe breakup sex is the best."

"I'm not one of those people," he told her and took back his hands.

Another woman might have reacted as if slapped in the face. That wasn't Simone's style. She rolled with whatever life threw at her. They kept on meeting at breakfast, and their sexual standoff became a running joke on Simone's part. "Why are you so stubborn? I've never met a man this difficult to seduce. It's as frustrating as your refusal to pose for me or to visit the Alhambra."

"I'm happy to take you to the Alhambra. Maybe after you see it, you'll agree to stay on."

"Fat chance."

"The invitation is open-ended."

"So's my invitation."

"Hope it's not a deal-breaker that Blessed will be visiting the Alhambra with us. Now that he has a bit of money, he could go there on his own, but I promised to keep him company."

"You're such a sweetheart," Simone said, half in mockery, half in melancholy.

• • •

They set out in unseasonable warmth for the steep uphill climb. It was Holy Week, a fact neither of them was aware of until they noticed penitents in white robes and hoods like Klansmen parading through the streets. Prayers and hymns of praise echoed around them. Strong men advanced in baby steps with a statue of the Virgin on their shoulders, negotiating the narrow entrance of a church as if gingerly inserting a model ship into a bottle.

In tan slacks and sturdy shoes, Simone strode along, drinking in the sweetness of mimosa blossoms. To escape the crush of traffic on Carrera de Darro, they crossed a rock-hewn footbridge to the south bank of the river. The path there was paved with black-and-white stones pieced together in a fan pattern that appeared to undulate under them. From a shaded corner, a grizzled beggar cried out to Simone, "*Me ahogaré en tus ojos.*"

"Do I dare ask what he's saying?"

"He says he'd be happy to drown in your eyes. In Granada, even street people are poets."

"Tell him he'll have to shower first."

"You Americans, always so clean and health conscious."

"I'll miss our banter."

"So will I."

"But when the *carmen* reopens," she said, "you'll have a fresh batch of smart-ass female artists to fool around with."

"I'm thinking of going in a different direction."

"And swear a vow of chastity?"

"I'm thinking of turning the residency into a refugee center. Blessed's already letting migrants bunk there. I might as well make it official."

Simone slowed down. She wanted to stop and talk this over. Paul kept walking.

"When did you lose your interest in the arts?" she asked, hurrying to catch up.

"It's more that I've gotten interested in other things."

"What do you expect to accomplish?" She sounded belligerently disbelieving.

"Maybe not all that much. But at least Blessed and his friends will have someplace safe and warm to sleep."

"How do you plan to pay the bills?"

Paul hadn't told her anything about his deal with the State Department, and he didn't do so now for fear of sounding like a jilted lover dangling wealth to convince Simone to reconcile. "There are outside sources of funding. International NGOs and charitable foundations."

"The line of applicants is a thousand miles long."

"'Cast bread upon the water,'" he said.

"And you get soggy bread."

"I won't waste time trying to convince you. It was hard enough to convince myself."

They swung uphill onto Cuesto de Gomerez, blending in with legions of tourists traipsing past souvenir shops and musical instrument stores. Guitars hung in the windows like hams in butcher shops. This was what used to put Paul off about the road to the Alhambra—the curb-to-curb kitsch, the bullfight posters, the souvenir mantillas and fake-leather wine botas, the kiosks thatched with overlapping guidebooks in Chinese, Arabic, Cyrillic, and Greek. The neighborhood seemed to have floated free from its Islamic attachments and become yet another sightseer's black hole, sucking in people, sucking away significance.

Now he embraced it all. Accepting the climb as a kind of pilgrimage, he fell in with travelers toting cameras and selfie sticks, backpacks and water bottles. The men had on ball caps and T-shirts emblazoned with team logos; the women carried banners identifying affinity groups. Youngsters sprinted ahead, while plodding oldsters depended on ski poles or canes and crutches. One crippled woman in a battery-powered wheelchair might have been a miracle seeker on the road to Lourdes.

Beyond a monumental arch, Paul and Simone detoured through a mossy forest of elms and ferns where the air was cooler, the light dense with pollen. "This is too much for me," Simone said, and leaned on the wall around a fountain.

"I warned you it would be a clusterfuck."

"I don't mean the people." She splashed water over her wrists. "It just hit me that in a couple of days, all of this will be gone, and so will you."

"No," he said quietly. "I'll be here, and so will Granada. You're the one who'll be gone."

Perspiration—or was it tears?—trickled down her cheeks. Paul waited for her, wanted her, to say more. When she didn't, he asked, "If you feel this way, why leave? I'd love you to stay."

"I don't understand you." She yanked sunglasses from her purse and masked her eyes. "Reopening the *carmen* as a refugee center is a crazy idea. You might as well start a monastery. Here you are worrying about Blessed and a billion refugees when you should be worried about yourself."

"I *am* worried about myself and about you. Your nosiness about the worst thing I ever did in my life set me thinking. I regret dozens of lousy decisions I've made out of convenience or cowardice."

Paul leaned beside her on the damp fountain. Amid the murmer of flowing water, with tree shade on their shoulders, he described how years ago, he had crouched, petrified, next to the Darro River while a little boy drowned. He wished he could see Simone's eyes instead of his own reflection mirrored in her sunglasses. Then again, he thought, her eyes might be full of contempt, and he was lucky not to face that as he fumbled to explain the boy's death as a prime example of his penchant for staying on the sidelines, observing yet uninvolved.

"That's terrible," Simone said.

"Yeah, that's what it was."

"I mean terrible that as a kid, you had to go through such an experience."

"I didn't have to go through it. I could have dived in. But I was scared."

"Of course you were scared. Who wouldn't be? The boy's mother must have been out of her mind with fear. Otherwise she'd have jumped into the river herself. Didn't that ever occur to you?"

"But you understand, don't you, why I can't bear to behave like that again?"

"Blessed's not drowning," she said. "Tahar wasn't drowning."

"You're being too literal."

"No, you are. You're acting like there's something you can do when there's nothing to be done. For all you know, there was nothing you could do that day at the river. The boy was probably already dead when his mother begged you to help."

"But Blessed's alive." Paul stood up and extended a hand to help Simone to her feet. "And he's waiting for me."

From a distance, the Alhambra appeared to be a stout fortress of stone, indestructible, impervious to time. But as Simone and Paul approached its lower reaches, it seemed as fragile as the sugar sketch on their morning coffee. Mortar had melted away, exposing the crude concrete blocks of its foundations. Without constant upkeep the grand landmark would crumble like a sandcastle.

Dwarfed by the Gate of Justice, Blessed was wearing new clothes. Or rather new old clothes from a charity shop. After weeks of regular meals, he had lost his starved-scarecrow look. He fluffed his yellow-tinted cornrows and said, "*Rubio*," just as he had the day he had first met Simone. He shook her hand, kissed his fingers, and pressed them to his heart. Then the three of them passed under the arch.

Grave and reverent, Blessed walked the grounds of the Alhambra as if on a personal hajj, an alternative to Mecca. Around him, cameras clicked and flashed. Visitors shouldered closer to squeeze into a picture. Others scooted aside to keep from intruding on someone else's selfie. Blessed remained apart, ignoring the hornet-fizz of guide-speak audible through earbuds.

The crowd flowed along on a river of languages whose distinct currents merged into what might have been a universal grammar. The three of them advanced toward the Alcazaba, where a

Japanese model in a white wedding dress posed for a professional photographer. Her makeup was as pale as a Kabuki dancer's. A crew of security guards held back the gawkers who snapped shots of the photographer shooting the woman.

At a parapet, Paul, Simone, and Blessed peered out over a rippling expanse of red tile roofs that sloped down to the Darro, then slanted up through the Albaicín. In the hieroglyphic scrim of TV antennae and satellite dishes, Paul succeeded in locating his *carmen*, his repaired querencia rising above the dice-scatter of cube-white houses.

As they climbed down from the parapet, he translated the lines of poetry carved on a marble plaque: "'Give him alms, woman / For there is nothing in life, no nothing / so sad as to be blind in Granada.'"

Simone slipped her hand out of Paul's. "I've had it."

"Like to rest in the shade again?"

"I'm heading back to the hotel."

"You haven't seen anything yet."

"I've seen enough."

"But I promised Blessed. This means a lot to him."

"What's it mean to you?"

"Look, if you really want to discuss that, it's a big subject. We'll have to do it later."

"I've talked enough. I'm leaving."

"I'll get you a taxi."

On tiptoes, she kissed his cheek. "Don't bother. I'll find my way."

Paul watched her descend the esplanade toward the Gate of Justice. If he expected her to pause and glance back, like the Moor exhaling a last sigh, he was mistaken. And if she hoped he would rush after her, she was wrong too. Once she was out of sight, Paul and Blessed joined the line leading to the Nasrid Palace.

Inside, where one might expect awe and worshipful silence to supplant the babble of guides and idle conversation, the acoustics of the contained space multiplied the racket. No single voice or word stood out. There was only a tide of unintelligible noise boiling along like the Arabic script around the walls that to an untutored eye might be mistaken for nothing more than snakes or flowers. Following in Blessed's footsteps, Paul let go, no longer resisting the chaos, entering it, borne along toward the Court of the Lions.